John Kay

Biography of the Rev. William Gundy

For Twenty Years a Minister of the Methodist New Connexion Church...

John Kay

Biography of the Rev. William Gundy
For Twenty Years a Minister of the Methodist New Connexion Church...

ISBN/EAN: 9783337016234

Printed in Europe, USA, Canada, Australia, Japan

Cover: Foto ©Raphael Reischuk / pixelio.de

More available books at **www.hansebooks.com**

BIOGRAPHY

OF THE

REV. WILLIAM GUNDY,

FOR TWENTY YEARS A MINISTER OF THE METHODIST
NEW CONNEXION CHURCH IN CANADA.

BY

REV. JOHN KAY.

ALSO, AN INTRODUCTION TO THE WORK, BY THE REV.
JAMES CASWELL, AND THE SERMON PREACHED AT
HIS FUNERAL BY THE REV. JAMES M'ALISTER,
PRESIDENT OF THE CONFERENCE.

TORONTO:
JAMES CAMPBELL & SON.

MDCCCLXXI.

TO THE READER.

T is recorded by the wise King of Israel, "The memory of the just is blessed." The man of holy life and earnest labor thus "being dead yet speaketh." How often, while perusing the biography of some well-known child of God, has the arrow of conviction pierced deep into the heart of the sinner, or the thrill of joy filled that of the believer with unspeakable comfort, while from its depths there was sent on its heavenward flight the language of gratitude and praise? Here is supplied a means by which a good example may be kept perpetually before the world; and, as it "speaks louder than precept," a valuable source of instruction is constantly furnished.

It appears to the writer of these unpretending pages, that the memory of our fathers should be kept in some substantial form, that we, our children, and our children's children, may have the benefit of their influence.

Some of our best and most readable books, especially to the young, are those of biography. They are calculated to open up to us the home life of a man, in which we are likely to find a lesson for more than one circumstance of our own.

When a good man dies, we are generally led to look upon the event as a calamity to us, a serious loss to the neighbourhood where he has lived—to the church, and to the family. Yet, by preserving the memory of such, the loss will be considerably diminished, and "the memory of the just" will be blessed to us. We are far from supposing that, because a friend, therefore we should rush into print, and make every possible effort to canonize an unfaithful man ; and we are as far from thinking it just, to ourselves, our children, or the Church, to refuse the reproduction of a life which cannot fail to be of service to us all. Nor does it seem a reason of sufficient importance because a man was not wonderfully distinguished for surpassing eloquence in the Pulpit, or at the Bar, or on the floor of the Senate, that, therefore there is nothing in his life worth retaining.

One of the most distinguishing traits in the character of a man is simple, undisguised, yet unfeigned, goodness of heart and life ; and perhaps it is not going too far, or implying too much of condemnation towards our common humanity, to say that this is one of the rarest accomplishments of the present age, and therefore worthy of being preserved.

The subject of these pages was not a great man, in the popular sense of the term. He was no illustrious military general, no nation's favorite poet, no burning seraph whose overpowering eloquence moved the nations, but an humble Christian—an every-day working and successful Methodist preacher, whose noblest memorial is the remembrance of his holy and useful life. His military ambition was that he might be a faithful "soldier of the Cross," his poetry the ringing harmonies of the Bible, and his only eloquence the well-known and oft-repeated Gospel epitome, "God so loved the world, that He gave His only begotten Son, that whosoever believeth in Him should not perish, but have everlasting life."

To continue his life of faith and love amongst us, is the only apology offered for presenting this little book to the public, and especially to the Church in which he lived, labored, and died.

No one can be more painfully conscious of its many literary defects than the writer; but the limited space of time in which the work is to be done, and the numerous duties involved in the charge of a circuit, forbid that it should be otherwise than imperfect. That its perusal may be blessed to your spiritual profit, and that its circulation may result in glorifying God, is the earnest prayer of

Yours affectionately,

JOHN KAY.

WATERDOWN, ONT.,
April 5th, 1871.

INTRODUCTION.

BIOGRAPHY, taken in its widest sense, is generally a very entertaining and instructive species of history. Most countries have produced it. Its first composers were the minstrels. The exploits of the chiefs were the subject of their song. They were most extravagant in the praise of their heroes—exalting them to demigods ; they represented them as achieving what was far beyond the reach of human ability. This was the fabulous age of biography, when nothing was too marvellous for credulity. Plutarch, who flourished in the second century, was the first to give to biography the place it now occupies among the departments of literature.

During the dark ages, in the hands of the monks, it lost its former rank, and was enlisted in the service of a gross and vile superstition. The subjects were Popish saints, whose only title to notoriety was their cunning, hypocrisy, and intrigue. But the truest, purest, most beautiful and influential biographies are those which have been given to the world by the true Church of Christ. No branch of Christian literature has been more acceptable to the

Church—been more extensively read—or exercised a more powerful influence for good. Next to the Bible, we know of no book better calculated to awaken and foster a fervent, active, generous piety, than a well written memoir of a pure and useful Christian. The life of a truly good man exhibits the beautiful foliage **and rich** fruit which the "seed of the kingdom" is capable **of** producing. Thus does it demonstrate the truth, purity and power of the Word of God. It presents to us the marble of human nature in the rude, unsightly block, and then the Divine artist in the use of Gospel instruments shaping it, till at length it assumes the fair proportions, graceful contour, and lovely features of the Divine ideal. It exhibits to us the Christian, as a babe, taking his first tottering steps in the way of life ; and then, in maturer years, with head erect, robust frame and vigorous limb, climbing life's rugged heights, battling successfully with his foes, and pressing forward, with light heart and lion courage, towards the house of many mansions—the home of his Father, God. It shows us the Christian passing through the process of purification—the gold having much alloy put into the furnace ; subjected to the influence of disappointment, loss, suffering and sorrow—the fuel which the Divine spirit usually employs to refine the ransomed spirit, and fit it for the highest service of the heavenly world. We see how well the true gold of Christian faith and patience stands the fiery ordeal, and then the tried ones come forth as gold seven times purified.

Christian biography exposes to view the moral weakness and sinward tendency of corrupt human nature, and, at the same time, the mighty forces of grace triumphing over such weakness, and overcoming the natural bias of the soul—leading the man onward and upward to perfection of moral principle and practice—and thus fitting him for the service, the song, and the rapture of Heaven. In a word, it is a literary panorama, in which the Christian pilgrim is made to pass before you, from his escape from the city of destruction till his triumphant entrance into the celestial city. Such literature cannot but be influential for good when the subject is worthy of portrayal, and the portrait is accurately drawn.

In such kind of literature, thank God, the Methodist Church is rich. No branch of the Church of Christ, we believe, is richer. It was the shrewd, grateful, exultant remark of the apostle of Methodism—" Our people *die* well." This was evidence that they had lived well—that their lives had been pure, exemplary, and useful.

The thrilling memoirs of the Wesleys—the lives of such holy men as Fletcher, Bramwell, Stoner, Smith, our own Barker, Waller and Allin, in the ministry ; and such men as Carvosso, Hick, and the Cornish miner amongst the laity, demonstrate the soundness of Methodistic faith, the fine adaptation of its means of grace to the cultivation of the deepest piety; and the free scope its institutions and varied plans of usefulness afford for the exercise of all the talent it can command. My esteemed brother Kay has, in the following memoir, added another to the list of these Christian heroes. The venerable subject of this memoir, though not a star of the first magnitude in the spiritual heavens, was nevertheless a "shining light"—one whose unselfish nature, beautiful harmony of spiritual development, humble, plodding industry in the work of God, and undying attachment to our beloved Church, cannot fail to render a biography interesting, instructive and useful to all readers, but especially to the members of our connexion.

Though not converted amongst us, he, by a course of rather singular circumstances, became one of us ; admirably defended and advocated our polity ; laboured hard and long to promote our interests ; and dying, bequeathed us the rich legacy of an unspotted reputation, and the influence of a life entirely devoted to his sacred calling. His spiritual family amongst us, in the aggregate, is, doubtless, large ; and of those that sprang from his loins, three sons are amongst our most honoured and useful ministers.

The first time the writer of this sketch saw him was more than twenty years ago, on a Sabbath morning, mounted on his faithful steed, cautiously passing over a rough crossway in the Township of Brock, to a distant appointment. We were much struck with his venerable and saintly appearance. Conspicuously did he then bear the stamp of an intelligent, upright and earnest man. Such was the first impression he made on our mind—an impression which a long and very intimate acquaintance only served to justify and deepen. During the year we travelled together on the Middleton circuit—a year, in most respects, distressing to him—one that must have severely tried his faith and patience—though realizing, as he must have done, the decay of his vital power—we never knew him shrink from duty. Nothing but an actual impossibility prevented him from fulfilling his engagements.

Father Gundy was a Methodist of the original stamp—one of a race which is fast disappearing,—a man whose preaching was not "in the enticing words of man's wisdom," but was "in the demonstration of the spirit, and with power." In a simple, clear and forcible manner, he laid open the plan of salvation ; in a very lucid and instructive way he expounded those great doctrines which the early Methodist preachers brought so frequently before their hearers, and which must ever form the groundwork of true religion. He never lost sight of Rowland Hill's three R's—Ruin by the Fall—Redemption by Christ—Renewal by the Divine Spirit. He never aimed at high things. He had no wing for the region of philsophy or abstruse science. No disposition to enter the pulpit with a bouquet of flowers to exhibit to his people, culled from the gardens of human genius and eloquence. No. He knew his people needed the living bread, and he sought to feed them from the storehouse of God's Word, with food convenient for them ; and many who sat under his ministry were led to bless God for such supplies. Dear old servant of Christ, he has ascended on high in the chariot of salvation. May his mantle rest on the shoulders of his sons, and may they be a thousand times more useful than he.

May the following tribute of filial piety and devout expression of gratitude to the giver of all good, be read with interest and profit by many, and be instrumental in bringing much glory to God.

JAMES CASWELL.

CAVANVILLE, Dec. 13th 1870.

CONTENTS.

BIOGRAPHY

OF THE

REV. WILLIAM GUNDY.

CHAPTER I.

HIS PARENTAGE, EDUCATION, APPRENTICESHIP, AND CONVERSION.

ELIZA MATHEWS, born about one hundred and twenty-five years ago, amongst the beautiful scenery of a rural part of King's County, Ireland, was the honored mother of the subject of this memoir. He was her only child. Of his father—William Gundy—who was also a native of King's County, very little is now known, save that he was a farmer and belonged to a family of several brothers, all following a similar occupation. They were all members of the Established Church. In that early day Methodism was little known in Ireland, excepting as a by-word or a subject

B

for ridicule or scorn.   The father and uncles of Mr.
Gundy, although living in the midst of a hot-bed **of**
Roman Catholicism, were staunch Protestants.   Perhaps
the opposition to which they were subjected resulted in
trying their faith, **and attaching them** more firmly to the
church, in the bosom of which they were born, and in the
principles **of which they were nurtured.**   By some coincidence of circumstances, regarded by them as wonderfully
Providential (as such things are generally considered by
youthful lovers) William Gundy and Eliza Mathews became
acquainted, **and their** acquaintance ripened into affection.
After some time they found their way to the altar, and in
the words of the service, **made sacred by** the hoary years
of time, "pledged their **faith either to** other," and were
fairly launched, **with,** perhaps, ordinary prospects for a
successful voyage, on the great ocean of human life.   **For**
many years they lived and loved together ; but no innocent prattle of the babe was heard.   The monotony **of**
living and loving alone was unbroken until the expiration
of the twentieth year of their married life, when the
subject of this memoir was born.   Like Samuel of old, he
was no doubt the child **of** many prayers and many hopeful thoughts, and, like him, he seems to have been **given**
to the Lord from his birth.

His parents, being members of the Church of England,
took their child, an infant of days, for baptism, and his
name was called William, after his father.   When William
was five years of age his father was removed by death,
through that lingering but no less fatal disease, consump-

tion. His mother was now left alone, with her only child, to conduct the business of her farm, and to make her way along as best she could in the weary weakness of widowhood. She was a woman of noble spirit and of sterling religious principle, but as yet, the religion of morality was the best she knew. The prayer-book and the catechism were familiar to her, and the Bible was interpreted in their light. It was her constant care that her child, who, under God, was to be her earthly stay, should be thoroughly instructed in the imperishable truths of religion. As nearly as I can gather—for no diary was kept, or written data can be found, from which to draw—she disposed of her small farm and effects, and invested the money for her support, and for the education and maintenance of her dearly loved son.

Methodism was then beginning to exert quite an influence amongst the people of that part of Ireland; and she took her boy, then a mere child, regularly every morning and evening to prayer-meetings held by these revivalists of Christian earnestness and love.

During all the years of his adult life, Mr. Gundy remembered with gratitude the earnest fervour and faithfulness of his mother's prayers in his behalf. He particularly remembered her oft repeated prayer, that the Lord would keep him from "bad company," and the ruinous influence of evil of all kinds. Thus she demonstrated to him, at least, that her morality had more of real religion in it than that ordinarily possessed and practised in those days. Her church, her catechism, and her book of com-

mon prayer, brought her into more or less familiarity with
the throne of grace. There is a great deal of real religion
even in this wholesome restraint upon natural evil, and
much to prompt the soul in its earnest yearnings to commit itself in trust to the guidance and government of the
divine unseen.

It was so in the case of Mr. Gundy's mother ; in evil
restrained and good cultivated, she imparted a large share
of her character to her son.

Mr. Wesley's head had been silently resting for five
years in the tomb, in old City Road Chapel, and his friend
and co-worker, George Whitfield, had already been in
glory twenty-five years, when the subject of this memoir
was born. He was not designed to take the leading part
of either of these men, but Methodism was to have in him
a firm adherent and a faithful friend.

He was born on Sabbath morning, the 10th of May,
1795, and while the bells were ringing for church service.
Mr. Wesley's name was still fresh in the memory of his
followers, and his mantle had fallen upon many of them,
when his zeal and faithfulness reproduced had sent them
into this Popish part of the Emerald Isle. Amongst the
number were the names of Gideon Ouseley, Charles Gra-
ham, William Hamilton, William Riley and Andrew Tay-
lor. Methodism was then growing into a power in England and America ; and in Ireland there were beginning
to be seen evidences of her soul-saving ministrations.

William began to go to school at a very early age. It
was not possible that a parent who loved him with an af-

fection so strong, and viewing his true interest as she did, could neglect so important a matter as his secular education; while, with all the tender earnestness of a fond mother, she scrupulously attended to his religious training. Schools were not then as effective or as accessible as in these highly-favoured times, and in this comparatively new country. At that time, if parents wished to educate their children, they were compelled to make a strong effort, and often submit to no ordinary sacrifices, in order to confer this lasting benefit upon their offspring. Almost, therefore, before he was mentally or physically qualified, William was sent to the nearest school. He soon showed an aptitude to learn, and, from the tenderest of years, began the training which was to fit him, first for his mercantile life, and afterwards was to be of service to him as a watchman on the walls of Zion. I have often heard him remark that he should never forget his first teacher. Her diminutive stature had merited for her the cognomen of " Peggy-the-Pie," and the earnest care she took of her pupils resulted in engraving her name indelibly upon their hearts. Well nigh four score years had rolled away, when, in conversation with him, he referred to her name. Yet it must not be supposed that her method of training was anything like that of the present day, and under *our* excellent common school system. She was probably a lone woman, who taught a school by the wayside. But even if this were the case, her kindness of heart and conduct much endeared her to the children, and this was quite an exception to the general rule in that country. It is a remarkable fact, in the history of schools in Ireland, that the teachers were extremely severe. They seemed to think that the most effective way to communicate instruction, and to make it stick, was to soften the skull, or blister the skin, with some horrid instrument of torture. It was cruel, very cruel, thus to abuse helpless children, in the hope of making them bright in intellect or tenacious in memory. Perhaps it was what he saw of this practice in some of his earlier schools, and its influence upon his young mind, that led him on one occasion to take great delight in beating out the brains of a neighbour's pig, which had strayed from home, and was luxuriating on the dung-hill. This was his first, and, I think, his only act of cruelty; and this itself was done more from the innocent ignorance of childhood, resulting from the forcible example of some of his teachers, than from any inherent cruelty. So imperfect was the entire system of education then, especially in the lower schools, that the teachers often had more real interest in lining their own pockets than in storing the minds of their children with knowledge. The children were often mere slaves to perform some physical labor, from which the teacher was to receive an income. As an evidence of this, we are informed that one of William's teachers kept his scholars regularly, a certain portion of the day, "footing turf"—an operation connected with the preparation of the fuel generally used, and from which work the teacher enjoyed a snug little supplement to his salary. Whether it was through the thoroughness of the teaching he received, or

in spite of its inefficiency, I know not, but he became
very well grounded in the rudiments of an English education. For the period of a few years we can find no trace
of his earlier history. Whether he was kept at school, or
was engaged in some branch of business, it is now impossible to determine, and perhaps it would not affect our
narrative to any considerable extent to know. We next
find him, in the year 1811, a youth of sixteen years, ap-
prenticed to a Mr. Wilson, a general merchant, of the
Town of Tullamore, King's County. This Mr. Wilson
was an upright man, and, conducting his business upon
strictly honest and honourable principles, was no stranger
to the pleasures and encouragements of success. This
inexperienced youth was not long in finding way to the
confidence and esteem of his employer, and he also made
good proficiency in the study of his business. Mr. Wilson,
after a short time, took the new apprentice into his confidence, and, relying upon his judgment and skill, soon began the practice of taking him to Dublin to assist in the
selection and purchase of goods, and from this time became his very intimate and true friend. Although Mr.
Wilson died in early life, he left behind him, for his family, the competency earned by honest toil and care, and,
better still, he entailed to them the priceless legacy of a
good name. He had two sons, of whom I have often
heard Mr. Gundy make honorable mention, and these became ornaments of their religious profession amongst the
Methodists. They afterwards emigrated to Canada, where
one of them, at least, Mr. John Wilson, became quite

eminent for his learning, and has held for many years a professorship in Victoria College, Cobourg, where he is still exercising the functions of his office, and has long labored as a faithful, effective and humble local preacher.

It was while in the employ of Mr. Wilson that Mr. Gundy, then a dark-haired, ruddy-countenanced young man, became converted to God, and soon graduated to the position of a diligent and acceptable local preacher amongst the Methodists. His conversion was, under God, brought about by the following circumstance :—One day, while attending to his duties at the store, Edward Divine, an eccentric yet very earnest and successful preacher, came in, and putting his hand upon Mr. Gundy's head, gave utterance to the thrilling language, " It is a great pity that such a head should burn in hell to all eternity!" Such a statement startled him, and led to his first very strong feelings concerning his spiritual condition. It will not be difficult to gather from the conduct of this preacher, the kind of men so very often in those days, and in many subsequent to that time, made instrumental in the conversion of souls. His views of **future** punishment evidently implied the existence of a material fire, as the sight of Mr. Gundy's head of fine, dark hair led to the strange statement mentioned above. It may seem singular that such an utterance should so alarm the conscience and lead to conversion; but God uses a variety of means by which to accomplish His great purposes. The thunders of Sinai and the love of Calvary are both used successfully, and God is glorified

thereby. Happy is the preacher who knows how and
when wisely to use either or both of these methods. At
first Mr. Gundy was led to serious reflection, and, while
under the present impulse, the promise was extorted that
he would, on the following Sunday, attend the class-
meeting. He kept his promise faithfully, and when the
morning came he was found amongst the people of God,
and he was very much surprised at what he heard and
saw.

He was fairly " terrified," to use his own language, " at
the reasons given by many of the members for their
conversion. The influence of these impressions he tried
to shake off. The ideas of a legal righteousness and
a religion which should consist of a cold morality seemed
to be instilled into his nature. He thought, Well, I have
not been very sinful after all ; and, like many others, he
tried to quiet his disturbed feelings, and silence the voice
of the monitor within, by making his case to appear as
good as possible in his own eyes. He contrasted himself
with others who were much more wicked, and tried to
feel as if he had little of which to repent. This was
very well for the first Sabbath ; the next he went for
a drive through the country. But he could by no means
find quiet or peace to his troubled mind, unconscious of
its danger until aroused by the unceremonious conduct
and language of Mr. Divine. This thought of " burning
in hell" he could not endure, and the more he revolved
it in his mind the more it troubled him. The consciousness of personal guilt seemed to grow stronger, and it .

only increased his anguish of soul. For weeks this was his miserable experience, and, like many a promising young man before and many an one since, he was ready to cry in the emphatic language of Paul, "O, wretched man that I am! who shall deliver me from the body of this death?"

About the Christmas of 1814 or 1815 he found his way to a Methodist preaching place, and heard a Mr. Foot — one of Mr. Wesley's preachers — discoursing, probably upon the Nativity of Christ, when light streamed into his soul. He was led to see his salvation attainable only through faith in the Atonement. He saw, he trusted, and was saved; and from that hour he labored to show his love for Jesus, and to publish the merits of His death.

It is astonishing how very similar is the working of the human mind in all men, in the great struggle for that change of heart which can only be effected as the blood of Jesus is savingly applied by the Holy Ghost.

It is the same old, old story of several stages from guilt to pardon—the startling thought, then the calm reflection, and the difficulty increasing, until, loathing one's self, and forsaken of **all** comfort, the soul, as a last resort, and with a conscious sense of the extremity to which it is brought, reaches to the mercy seat crying, "None but Christ! none but Christ!" Of course the details of each man's conversion may differ somewhat from those of most others; yet, in the main, the great leading points in the struggle for life are the same, and prove beyond any reasonable doubt that the author of the work is the same in every instance.   How should this thought remind **us** that the happiness which we enjoy, and the heaven towards which we are travelling, are the common lot and common home of God's children.

How should these views of our great experience and our common interest bind Christians of all ages and of all churches together in one indissoluble bond of brotherhood and love.   This should put a successful end to all unlawful strife and unholy jealousies, and gradually lessen the lines of distinction between us, and make us all one as Jesus and his Father are one.

After his conversion he was wonderfully filled with the love of Jesus.   It was frequently his custom to repair to some secret place, and there, unseen by mortal eye, he would pour out his soul in prayer before God.

These were the days of his "first love," and full and sweet it was.   He often said to his friends, that so full was his soul with glorious peace, that he was sometimes compelled to turn, while waiting upon a customer, and wipe away the tears which the joy of a full heart had forced from his eyes.   The true believer will fully understand this when he remembers the well-spring of joy which religion forms within the heart.   Who that has truly tasted of the sweets of religion does not know the bliss of "first love?"   **I am** persuaded that there is nothing in all the range of personal experience which can in any way compare with it.   So gentle, and yet so rushing full; so satisfying, and yet creating such a thirst for

more ; so far above everything earthly, that the soul sings
in heavenly ecstasy,

> My God, I am Thine,
> What a comfort divine,
> What a blessing to know that my Jesus is mine !
> In the heavenly Lamb
> Thrice happy I am,
> And my heart it doth dance at the sound of His name.

> True pleasures abound
> In the rapturous sound,
> And whoever hath found it, hath paradise found.
> My Jesus to know,
> And feel His blood flow,
> 'Tis life everlasting, 'tis heaven below.

> Yet onward I haste
> To the heavenly feast !
> That, that is the fulness, but this is the taste.
> And this I shall prove,
> Till with joy I remove
> To the heaven of heavens in Jesus' love.

CHAPTER II.

SPIRITUAL ADVANCEMENT — EMPLOYED AS A LOCAL
PREACHER — INCIDENT AT OPEN-AIR PREACHING—
MR. WILSON, OF TULLAMORE.

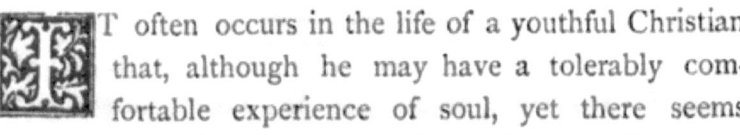T often occurs in the life of a youthful Christian that, although he may have a tolerably comfortable experience of soul, yet there seems an inward desire for some other evidence of acceptance with God. It was so in a limited degree with the subject of these pages. The deep things of God were working upon his mind, and he was desirous of a more full and clear token of the Spirit-Witness. One day, as he was walking along the road, quietly musing upon the subject of religion, and especially upon the great change which had been wrought within him, when the following passage came up before his mind with singular clearness and force: "God is love; and he that dwelleth in love dwelleth in God, and God in him." This fully set his mind at rest. He was satisfied that the highest and best quality of religion is love. This was to him the essence of true happiness, and became then, and was ever afterwards, the spring of his thoughts with God and his labors amongst men. No longer did doubts, like grim ghosts, haunt him by day or by night. No longer were fears and forebodings of ill his unpleasant companions. His experience thus became clear and satisfactory. This state

of things was strikingly characteristic of the early Methodists. I sincerely hope **we** are not in any measure de-
generating from this simplicity. It will be a sad day for
the Church of Christ should men forget or neglect **to**
realize fully a clear sense of the Divine approval.

> "I want the witness, Lord,
> That all I do is right,
> According to Thy will and word,
> Well pleasing in Thy sight."

At the request of the writer, Mr. Gundy furnished, in
a letter dated Omemee, 20th August, 1868, the following
facts regarding his conversion and early life; but it will
be seen at once that his memory even then had failed
him very much :—

"My mother was a God-fearing woman, and though
not fully **converted** till the close of her life, in her 96th
year, yet she would have me to seek the Creator. She
made it a particular point to bring me to the house of
prayer. She attended both the Methodist and English
churches. The first teacher that I **attended** was a **very**
small person, and nick-named Peggy-the-Pie. The next
teacher was a good man, and did all he could to reform
his scholars; the last was a most excellent teacher,
although a Roman Catholic, and was a moral, good-
living man, all things considered.

"My conversion to God was about the year 1814,
when living with **Mr.** Wilson, a man of very extensive
mercantile business. And oh, what a time that was!
The whole town was stirred up—high and low, great and
small; and **numbers** became acquainted with God,

through Christ. There was a young man in the next store who united with me to hold prayer-meetings. We used to visit the poor and pray with them, and spend an hour or more on the Sabbath days in some backward place, and there and then pray with **and for** each other— that we might be strong in the Lord, and in the power **of** His might. I was not only justified, but certainly sanctified. Oh, how happy was I then ! What power I had with God! But, alas! my friend left me. He was a Quaker, or Friend, at first, and he went back; but his elder brother still, while he remained in the store, continued a faithful local preacher. They both removed—one to Birr and the other to Clonmel—and, if alive, are both rich. Their names were Samuel and William Fayle. From that time I had to creep on as I could. I promised to serve Mr. Wilson for five years, which I faithfully did, and spent six years afterwards, making it eleven years; and we had no bond on either side."

The above letter was left unfinished, and in eight days after a few lines were added; it was signed, and in due course found its way into my hands, An accident, to which reference is made towards the close of this book, I am persuaded, in some measure accounts for the discontinuance of the narrative.

Mr. Gundy at once connected himself with the Methodist church, and in assuming this new relation he became the subject of many trials. They came sometimes from quarters whence they were least expected. It was not *then* as fashionable as *now* to be a Methodist.

In order faithfully to continue amongst this people, a man must have a firm and decided mind, Churchmen, Roman Catholics, and men of no religious belief, stood in bold array to oppose and affright the youthful follower of Jesus.

His early zeal for Christ and love for souls soon impelled Mr. Gundy to take more than the ordinary stand against the ranks of sin, and he, giving promise of usefulness, was soon engaged as a local preacher. This was an employment in which he delighted. He began now to find the benefit of his early education, limited though it was, as we have previously shown. He entered right earnestly into the study of the Scriptures. The holy unction and love, to which we have referred, evidently qualified him for the duty; and that which was in any case a duty, became to him a delightful and exalted privilege. The Bible he took "as the man of his counsel and the guide of his footsteps," and it became the source of solid preparation for his work of saving men. As in most Methodist exhorters of that day, so in him—burning zeal for the glory of Christ was a leading feature of his life. He began to work in the Master's vineyard at a time when, in Ireland, Methodism was held in leading-strings by the *Church.* Then, it was a breach of Methodistic usage to allow preaching to be conducted at the time of church service. It was customary for the preachers breathing Mr. Wesley's spirit, and covered by his descended mantle, to wait with abated breath until the people were retiring from church service, and then, elevated a little from the ground, they would announce and begin to sing some beautiful and touching hymn to gain the attention, then a few words were offered in prayer, the text was announced, and a sermon, generally distinguished for holy fervour and power, was delivered. This was frequently done by both the itinerant and local preachers.

Early one beautiful Sabbath morning, in company with a young man by the name of Robert Stewart, with whom he had been acquainted from childhood, and to whom he was strongly attached—the more so because Robert, like himself, was a youthful follower of Jesus—Mr. Gundy started for a small village about two miles and a half from Tullamore, for the purpose of preaching the Gospel. On arriving at the village, he requested permission from a woman to preach in her house, but she refused, on the ground that it would interfere with the time of church service, and she did not like to offend the minister and the people of the place. They, however, were not long in finding some other way of gathering a congregation, as well as obtaining a place in which to preach. They resolved to stand near the door of the church, and, as the people were leaving for home, they might get a few moments hearing from them. In referring to this matter afterwards, Mr. Gundy said he was somewhat nervous at being brought so closely in contact with the church minister—a known opponent of the Methodists—and his legs trembled until his knees nearly smote together, at the thought of thus having to conduct religious worship

C

at a place where there were so few to sympathize with his object, and so many who would be likely to oppose him. He, a mere boy, would most likely be met and attacked by the officiating clergyman ; and the more he thought of the work the more he shrank from it.

He, however, soon resolved what to do, and repairing to an adjacent field he knelt down to wrestle with God in prayer. What a glorious place of refuge is the throne of grace, and how our fears fly and our souls attain confidence under the influence of heavenly help ! While thus engaged in the spirit of Jacob's importunity, like Jacob, he obtained the blessing, and his soul was filled to overflowing with the love of God. All his fears soon vanished, and he was strong to take up his cross.

It was the time of sacrament at the church, and as they were nearly through, Mr. Gundy arose and announced the hymn and Robert Stewart pitched the tune. Very soon the people came streaming from the church to see what this irregular proceeding could mean. In a short time nearly the whole congregation were outside the church, and the parsons—for there were two this day —left the service of the sacrament, because there were no subjects for communion, and they joined the people to listen to the youthful, but now fearless, preacher. I cannot now determine the text he took at that time, for his voice is for ever silent in death, and there are no means of obtaining this knowledge, yet it is enough to know that the Word was " with power, and in the demonstration of the Holy Spirit." Several were constrained to cry aloud for mercy, amongst whom was the woman who had refused them the use of her house. She was thoroughly convicted of sin, and was led to Jesus, in whose love she was made happy. These were not unfrequent scenes in the labors of the preachers, both local and itinerant. The clergyman, relieved of his congregation and having come to hear, was displeased, and began to threaten Mr. Gundy. All kinds of punishment were in store for him, on account of this *irregular* effort to save men; but after the heat of passion was passed, the matter was allowed to drop. Although those street services very often resulted so beneficially to many who attended them, it must be remembered that they cost their conveners much labor and self-denial. The preacher seldom found a congregation assembled from previous announcement, but he took his stand in some public place, and, while singing the hymn with which to begin the service, he thus collected his audience. The sound of singing would fall suddenly on the ear, alike of the listless wanderer and the bustling man of business, and through these means many were attracted to the spot —both Protestant and Papist—who sometimes listened attentively, often otherwise. Such meetings were denounced by those who were called the regular clergy, and were styled irregular, factious, and such like; but it must have been a source of great consolation in after years to those who held them, to know that there were men, influential and useful in the church, and many more in heaven, who first felt the power of Gospel truth at those services. The men who held those meetings were noble successors of Wesley and Whitfield, and were honored and distinguished by God in this work. While the Church of England and the Church of Rome were contending about Apostolic succession, and were striving for the "foremost seat," and while they were united to afflict and persecute the Methodists, these men of God were really doing a noble work in saving souls, and in laying the foundation of a system of religious agency which would employ its forces, not for the glory of man, but of God. From year to year Mr. Gundy continued those services, during which time he was still in the employ of Mr. Wilson before named. Mr. Wilson was not a Methodist himself, but, his wife being one, he was led to regard them somewhat favorably, and he was not slow to perceive that, at least, no harm was done to his business in consequence of the meetings held by Mr. Gundy in the adjacent towns and villages. It was often remarked that, after some of these services, the people would find him out at the store, and, refusing to be attended by anyone else, would wait their turn to be served by the man who, on the previous Sunday, had pointed them to the Lamb of God.

It is to be hoped that, rude and unlettered as many of them were, they had been taught to know that a man of true religion was a man of honesty and fairness in dealing. He wore a remarkably honest and open face, and thus nature and grace had conspired to qualify him both for his secular business and for his spiritual toil — for his

Sunday and his week-day labor. After a while Mr. Wilson began to give him extended privileges in these things, and furnished him with a pony, all saddled and bridled and beautifully groomed, by which to make his journeys to and from the Sabbath meetings. For the term of eleven years he served Mr. Wilson faithfully ; and I have often heard him speak of his old employer in the very highest terms of respect and esteem.

Mr. Wilson was a member of the Established Church, but perhaps the fact of his wife being a true Methodist may in some measure account for his evident leaning towards them, and may also furnish a reason for the fact that the two sons before named became firmly attached to this branch of the Church of Jesus Christ. There appears to me scarcely any limit to a mother's influence over her children. Always with them in their young days, and while their minds are plastic, to mould and fashion them according to her will, she makes their lives the counterpart of her own. At the expiration of Mr. Gundy's term of service with Mr. Wilson, he removed from Tullamore to Castlecomer, and began business for himself. During all this time he was unremitting in his duties as a local preacher, and this in addition to his business duties kept his time and mind fully occupied. In this service for the Lord, Robert Stewart very frequently accompanied him, and often rendered good help, especially in the singing department. I must not forget to say that, during his stay of eleven years at Tullamore, he had procured a place of residence for his mother in the same town, so that he could always be near her.   No human being could in his affections supplant his mother. **She** was a good mother, and he was a dutiful and affectionate son.

CHAPTER III.

HIS MARRIAGE — MRS. GUNDY'S PARENTAGE — SETTLE-
MENT IN BUSINESS—REMOVAL, BY DEATH, OF HIS OLD
FRIEND, MR. WILSON, ETC.

OW very true it is that "man never continueth in one stay." His life is the scene of constant change in the physical as well as in the intellectual and moral world.

It cannot be said of any of us, he is just where he was ten years ago. Time carries us all along the changeful road of life. He brings the babe of yesterday up to the boy of to-day, and this boy he pushes forward to manhood, with wonderful speed. As is the case with most men, in this particular, so was it with the subject of this little book. Only a short while ago, we were looking at him, "the only son of his mother, and she a widow," now he has passed along to the young man of twenty-seven years, and few more vigorous in body or brain.

Naturally good looking, his urbanity of manner and kindliness of heart, made him a general favourite. The greatest change of all his life, save his conversion, was soon to take place ; he was about to choose a companion who should share with him the joys and trials of life.

The ways of Providence are often very peculiar. So it would seem in this case ; so in most cases we find it, when after the lapse of a few years, we look back over

the way the Lord hath led us. Without any particular
anxiety about taking to himself a wife, the circumstances
now to be narrated, took place. Some time in the year
of our Lord, 1821, a daughter of Mr. John Bradley, of
Castlecomer, County of Kilkenny, came to Tullamore
on a visit to her sister—the wife of the Rev. James Sterling, Wesleyan Minister. While on this visit at her
brother-in-law's house, Miss Bradley saw Mr. Gundy for
the first time, as he was officiating in the pulpit of the
Methodist church.

Shortly afterwards they became acquainted, and Miss
Bradley, finishing the visit with her sister, soon returned
to Castlecomer. Some months afterwards, Mr. Gundy,
in company with his friend, Robert Stewart, paid a visit
to Castlecomer, and found it very convenient to make a
call at Miss Bradley's residence, just for acquaintance
sake.

I presume that in most cases of true love, there is more
or less of romance about the introduction and first acquaintance, and, of course, something wonderfully providential in all the subsequent stages of their relation.
This case was in no way exceptional to the general rule.
Mr. Gundy sought an interview and obtained it. After
the usually numerous and peculiar preliminaries, the bond
of their union was sealed by the Church clergyman, Rev.
Mr. Stone, on the third day of November, 1822. This
day was the Sabbath, the place, the Episcopal Church of
Castlecomer. At that time, the Methodist preachers were
not allowed to perform the marriage ceremony. Mrs.

Gundy's father, John Bradley, was born in the County of Kilkenny, on a farm, about two miles from Castlecomer. This farm, it is supposed, was sold to Mr. Bradley's father, for two and six pence per acre, by King William of England, with whom he came over at the formation of the English colony there. At his father's death, Mr. Bradley entered into possession of the property, and adding to this an interest in a coal-mine in the neighbourhood, he was engaged in extensive operations, and was favoured with the encouragements of success.

He was twice married. His first wife, Miss Wright, of the county of Kilkenny, was an excellent woman, and an earnest Methodist. She died suddenly, at an early age, leaving him with four children—two sons and two daughters. His second wife, was Miss Ellen Odlum, with whom he lived many years, until his death. She survived him nine years, and was the mother of twelve children—seven sons and five daughters. She was also a pious and intelligent Methodist. Mrs. Gundy was the first child by this last marriage. In both father and mother, she saw the graces of the Christian exemplified. Their house was always a home for the preachers, where everything was done, which affectionate regard could suggest, to make them comfortable, and help to lighten the labor of their hands.

Parental example is always a fruitful source of instruction ; but, especially in those times, the persecutions, to which Methodist parents were exposed, resulted in exhibiting the practical character of their religion, and in stimulating the children with a holy enthusiasm to become also followers of the meek and lowly Jesus. That which Mrs. Gundy saw in the spirit and conduct of her parents, gave her naturally a warm heart towards the Methodist preachers, and led to her many acts of kindness towards **them** in after years.

Eliza Bradley—now Mrs. Gundy—was by no means a hindrance to her husband either in business or religion, but was a great help to him in both. Entering into the **spirit** of his business, as of his religion, she became in the truest sense of the term "an help meet for him."

She was soundly converted to God when fifteen years of age—about the year 1815. In company with the family, she was accustomed to attend the Methodist preaching service at the Colliery, about two miles from Tullamore, somewhere near her father's farm. She was an attentive listener, even at that early age, and was led to a conviction of her sinful state while listening to a sermon from the Rev. John Stewart, Wesleyan preacher. He was preaching from a text in *Luke* xi., 21, 22. "When a strong man armed keepeth his palace, his goods are in peace: but when a stronger than he shall come upon him, and overcome him, he taketh from him his armour wherein he trusted, and divideth his spoils." And, while **he** endeavoured to show the weakness of the mightiest when contending with the almighty strength of God, the word was applied with power to her soul.

She saw the hopelessness of her case as a sinner, and was led to look to the strong for strength. From this time she was anxiously enquiring for the Saviour of sinners; and while earnestly looking to heaven for a consciousness of pardon, she was not disappointed, for coincident with the effort of her soul in faith, came the light and power of the Holy Ghost, and she was "healed from that very hour."

Surrounded as she was by those helps to religion, which the pious example of father mother and friends furnished, she daily grew in grace. How many young people would be saved from making shipwreck of faith and a good conscience if, when they were first brought to a knowledge of the truth, they were favoured with the surrounding atmosphere in which the children of God daily move. There is almost a moral certainty of success to those who are thus highly favoured. Alas, for those children who are compelled to serve God amidst the sinful influences, and surrounded by the pestilential clouds formed by the unholy lives of friends and near relatives! One may contend successfully against an occasional attack from without, but, especially in the case of the young, it is hard for them to travel heavenward while every moment the poison of sin is being infused by those who ought carefully to guard against anything so thoroughly calculated to ruin them. From day to day Miss Bradley moved forward in the heavenward journey; and now that she had entered life, with her heart linked in purest affection to that of her husband, she was prepared to help rather than hinder him in the work which, of all others, lay nearest his heart. Happy is the man who, in starting in

life, is blest with so congenial a companion. I often
think that the young of both sexes, especially the children
of Jesus, are not sufficiently careful to guard against being
"unequally yoked together." Two cannot walk safely
together except they are agreed; and it seems practically
impossible for two lives to become one unless their religious views and feelings are similar. In the case now
before us there was not merely mutual affection, as this is
generally understood, but this was heightened by the
sanctifying influence "of the love of Christ, which passeth
knowledge."

After their marriage, Mr. Gundy returned to Tullamore, and remained a month with his old employer. As
he had now determined to embark in business for himself,
he found it necessary to obtain his mother's money, which
had been invested with Mr. Wilson.

He received the value of the money in goods from
Mr. W., who also accompanied him to Dublin, and helped
him to as many more as would give him a fair stock with
which to begin trade. He fixed on Castlecomer as his
first place of business, and his mother, who had all along
been his constant care, was taken to live with them.

About six months after this Mr. Wilson was taken ill,
of that dreaded affliction, apoplexy, from which he never
rallied, but losing the use of his powers, as it were at
once, he gradually sank down into the tomb; and Mr.
Gundy was sent for to close up his business. As he had
lived at this place for eleven years, and having established
his reputation for honesty and business ability, there

was, perhaps, no one better qualified to undertake this task.

He felt the loss of Mr. Wilson very much. For years his daily counsellor, and being now suddenly taken away, he felt the stroke to be very severe indeed. One of his best friends was now gone, and his chief business prop being removed, he felt himself almost alone again in the world. But he had now come to man's estate, and to contend with the stern realities and overcome the sterner difficulties of life was to be his work ; and, after closing up the business of his old and tried friend, he repaired to Castlecomer, to exert every energy with dependence upon Divine Providence for the prosperity he desired ; and for some time he was singularly successful. Unlike too many of the merchants of his own or our time, he did not so engross himself in business as to leave no time or inclination for the more important affairs of his soul and the souls of others. He continued all this time a zealous and faithful local preacher, travelling many miles, and working very hard to publish abroad a knowledge of the sinners' Friend.

It is often very wonderful how Providence makes use of incidental circumstances, and what may appear to us unimportant matters, in order to further the ends of His cause. There was no very special reason why Mr. Gundy should settle in business in Castlecomer, save the fact that his wife's friends resided there, and it would be pleasant to be near them ; but after years revealed another and more important reason. There was a work before

him which he little expected, but from the performance of which he never shrank.

There was no Methodist church in the town, and in counsel with some of his friends, he saw it to be his duty to try, and, if possible, secure for the little "band of men whose hearts the Lord had touched," a place in which to worship God.

He interested himself in the work, and after much toil and responsibility, realized its completion. He undertook to solicit subscriptions in Castlecomer and the towns and villages around, and soon had enough money paid and promised to warrant him in beginning the erection of the house.

Emmerson Williams, a member of the Society, undertook the work of building; but, when it was about half done, he grew tired of the undertaking, and, from some reason or reasons unknown, left Mr. Gundy to finish as best he could. This was quite a blow for him, and no doubt produced a degree of discouragement for a time; but he was prompted to persevere, and persevere he did.

This Mr. Williams had as much right to bear a share of the responsibility of completing the work as Mr. Gundy, yet like many another timid man, he was more in love with self-ease and interest than with the material affairs of God's house; and Mr. Gundy was made to feel the unfaithfulness of human help, by being left alone with this great undertaking on his hands. He did not shrink, however, from the task. He paid the workmen regularly from his own pocket, every Saturday; and, after obtaining

the services of a Dublin architect, he had the satisfaction
of seeing the building completed. Another and unex-
pected difficulty now arose. A law had just passed the
Legislature **changing** the money from the Irish to the
English **method of** computing its value. This law had
the unhappy effect of lessening the value of the Irish
coin ; and, upon the strength of the law, the contractors
refused to accept their pay at the previous rates of value.
It will be clear that these men were bent on taking
the advantage of him, although they knew that his relation to the whole affair was disinterested, and arose from
feelings of purest benevolence.

The change **in** the money could not in any case make
any material difference, at least for some time, as it would
only be felt by those whose calling led them to transact
business in England. Mr. Gundy, therefore, allowed
them to sue him ; and the case came, in due course,
before the Courts. Strange as **it may** appear, some of
the Roman Catholic lawyers **of** the place undertook the
case for him; and, although considerable excitement **was**
necessarily caused by it, they were successful, **and** so he
was saved from no inconsiderable personal loss which would
otherwise, have been occasioned. It is somewhat strange
that those men should thus have undertaken to carry the
case through for him, when it was well known to them
that his influence was adverse to their Church ; and especially when the building erected through his efforts would
be a centre of influence all tending to neutralize the work
and prevent the spread of Roman Catholic influence in

the place.   This was to be the church of an open Bible;
and here the earnest preacher, whose "soul is on fire
with the love of men," would hold forth to all who might
come, both Papist and Protestant, the remedy for all soul
sickness, which is "Christ crucified."

Perhaps, however, they, like the great majority of
educated laymen in the Roman Catholic Church, took
little pains to inform themselves on the various questions
of religious belief.   This matter with them was probably
left with the priests and the various orders of ecclesiastics
to settle; while the law, and not the Gospel, should be
the source of their inspiration.   This is very often the
position taken by many, very many, of the educated
persons in Roman Catholic communities, and it only
makes the localities where they live the more inviting
fields for evangelistic effort.   The ignorant rabble, pre-
judiced against a man or a system without understanding
either, is certainly the least encouraging field for the
earnest follower of Christ.

"Ignorance is the mother of devotion," as practically
applied by Rome, has been the most successful means of
holding the poor deluded sons of men at a distance from
the light of truth; while their only hope has been in the
"infallibility" of the most fallible of all churches.   They
have thus been shut up in heathen darkness, and have
been daily employed in forging the chains of their own
bondage.   How sad it is to see men chained to any
system by the sheer fact of their own ignorance; but it
is worse to see men of education, upon whom the de-

velopment of truth in science and art and history may
have done much to raise them, still fastened, soul and
body, to a dangerous and false system of religion, with
no strong desire to examine the foundation of their vain
hope.

D

CHAPTER IV.

ENCOURAGEMENTS TO CHURCH BUILDING — A NEW
TRIAL — CARLO CIRCUIT — WILLIAM POOLE, OF
COOEN.

FTER much care and toil, which doubtless
caused him many anxious moments, as well
as sleepless nights, Mr. Gundy succeeded in
collecting all the money required for this disinterested
undertaking ; and, as the result, there has stood in Castlecomer for many years, and perhaps to this day, a comfortable stone church, dedicated to the worship of God, which
has been the spiritual birth-place of many souls, and which,
but for the untiring efforts of our subject, might never
have been there. Not the least important work of the
Christian man or minister, by any means, is the erection
of suitable places of worship where they are really needed.
This material means results in changing the field, or spot
where nature has sent forth her shoots, suggestive of the
supreme beneficence of her maker, into holy ground—
where Heaven and earth meet in the interchange of di-
vinest sentiments. Here the offended God, in yearning
pity, and offending man, in broken-hearted penitence,
meet ; and the place thus marked becomes the spot where
cluster our tenderest feelings and purest affections. Men
in the evening of life's day look back to it, and angels,
from their Heavenly home, look down upon it : and both

bless God that there human hearts were pardoned **and** purified, and the first stages of "a life of heaven on earth" begun. This church is a material monument to the zeal and faith of him of whose memory we cherish the fondest recollections.

If interests such as we have **described** belong to such an enterprise, who will question the **wisdom** of those thus employed, or who can define the limit of their pleasure? Like the house of Obed-edom, the Temple at Jerusalem, where the priest **approached** the mercy-seat; or like the latter **city, shining** in the rays of the risen sun of righteousness, or burning with the glory of Penticost,—such a place becomes the vestibule of Heaven, and it is cherished in memory by men through **time and** forever. The spiritual and the material **are** blended **with** the harmonies **of** Heaven. "Work done for **God, it** dieth not."

Some time before the opening of the **church at** Castlecomer, through a complication of adverse circumstances, Mr. Gundy was compelled to close his business operations in that town. A new trial awaited him. His business was extensively patronized by the men of the Colliery; but the work there failed to a considerable extent, and many of the men were forced to retrenchment in their expenditure. Just about this time, a new merchant opened a store in Castlecomer, and, having married a wealthy lady, and becoming suddenly possessed **of a** large quantity of ready money, began to make terms with these miners: so that, by charging **a** high figure for his goods, and by giving long credit, he succeeded in getting most

of their custom.   Difficulties seldom come single-handed,
and to the above may be added a circumstance which
also tended to lessen his business, and which arose chiefly
from a spirit of opposition to him as a Methodist.   This
came from a quarter least expected—from those who were
members of the English Church.   These men were vio-
lently opposed to the spread of Methodism ; and the prominent part which Mr. Gundy took amongst the Methodists subjected him to difficulties not only in his personal
associations, but to even greater in his commercial trans-
actions.   This matter of which we speak was more to be
deplored, from the fact that the Episcopal clergyman became the leading spirit in the opposition.   Lady Ormond,
a proprietress of large estates in that part of Ireland, had
been for some years accustomed to make an annual present of one hundred pounds' worth of kersies and blankets
to the poor.   For several years, Mr. Gundy succeeded in
satisfying the manager of her business with goods, at a low
price, and of good quality ; but for some reasons unknown,
only on the ground of his being a Methodist, this agent
was persuaded to have the business done by tender.   Of
course, this bore the aspect of fairness, and was quite a
plausible suggestion ; and it would have been, under
ordinary circumstances, a wise course.   But, under the
cloak of fair dealing, was evidently the hidden intention
of getting Lady Ormond's patronage from this young
Methodist merchant.   Mr. Gundy put in his tender, mark-
ing his samples as low as possible, in order to furnish a
good article ; but it seems as if some understanding was

entered into by the common opponents, for the trade was given to a man not at all engaged in the dry goods business only—as he would make the purchases to supply this order—and it was afterwards said that, to do so, he furnished an article much inferior to his sample. In this case, the poor were the sufferers, and the trade was taken from Mr. Gundy, who, by pressure of circumstances, was compelled to find some more inviting field for his occupation. It was not a very difficult matter, for one acquainted with the circumstances, to trace this whole affair to its origin, as it evidently arose from the inherent opposition of these men to Methodism ; and especially as this form of religious doctrine and practice interfered with the doctrinal views and shamed the spiritual indolence of the church people. The Rev. Mr. Despard, Church of England curate, thought to nonplus and entirely silence the Methodists, by establishing a weekly meeting in some private house, for the open discussion of general religious questions. At these meetings, any one could propose a subject for discussion on the next evening ; and, when it was agreed upon by the meeting, the matter was fixed, and all went home to prepare as well as possible for work. From the nature of the subjects often discussed, it was evident that the Episcopalians thought the Methodist doctrine easy to demolish, or the defenders of it perfectly powerless in their grasp. Many of the clergymen then, as now, were very zealous Calvinists, and lost no opportunity to promote the peculiar interests of this school. In his turn, Mr. Gundy proposed the question for discussion, and, on one particular occasion, named the "extent of the Atonement" as the subject for the following meeting, and it was agreed upon. There is little doubt but the Calvinistic party, especially as it was led by the minister, would readily accept such a subject, in full prospect of a victory. Mr. Despard and his friends strained **every** nerve to have present at the meeting as many clergymen and others as would be likely to render service to his side **of** the question. The controversy began, and the "universality" side was fully explained and defended by Mr. Gundy. He was met by the church party, and, in a hand-to-hand encounter, they proceeded for some time. Mr. Gundy was left chiefly alone, as the public defender of the doctrines of Methodism, in this as in other encounters. Yet we are by no means to infer that the rest of the Methodists were unacquainted with these doctrines or the scriptural arguments by which they were supported.

In those days, the followers of Wesley made it a matter of principle to be well read in doctrine. They were not only able to explain their views, but were very well qualified in a number of instances, to defend them. They were Methodists, not because it was fashionable, or in the **line** of popular applause, but because, **as** a matter of principle, they held truth and the privileges of the Gospel as more valuable than personal ease or temporal aggrandizement. This fact was brought out very strikingly at the meeting referred to, the result of which was entirely to defeat the object of the Calvinistic party; and, by clear scriptural proof, to demonstrate beyond a doubt the doctrine that "Jesus Christ, by the grace of God, tasted death for *every man.*" The clerical party were greatly chagrined at the success of these mere secularists, and, by resorting to such means as they could use, were determined to **compel,** if possible, Mr. Gundy to leave the place ; and what they could not do by fair argument, was effected by force of circumstances, brought about, to a considerable extent, by their influence. Mr. Gundy, being the leading spirit in the contest, was made the subject of heaviest attack, in which his opponents were compelled to leave the moral for the material argument. They left the true ground of all such questions, and settled, or tried to settle, the matter by removing the immediate cause of their greatest perplexity. It is very wonderful to what extent religious differences often lead ; and how very foolish are the men who allow themselves to be unduly excited in the interest of any sect, apart from higher and nobler considerations. There was no fault, in point of moral character, to be found in him of whom we write,—no blind opposition, **no bigoted** attachment to form,—but a constant, even life of faith and prayer, and an ever active determination to preach Jesus to the people. His religious influence must have been considerable at Castlecomer, and, personally, he was generally respected ; and the opposition to which he became subject was against his doctrinal views, and especially against Methodism, rather than against himself.

James Douglass was the Wesleyan preacher at Castlecomer when first they went to the place. I believe, at the next conference, James Olive was sent to the circuit. He soon formed an acquaintance with Mr. Gundy, and they became very intimate and firm friends. The circuit was called by the name of Carlo, at which place, about fourteen or fifteen miles from Castlecomer, the preacher resided. It took in a wide range of country, but principally included a number of villages; Baltonglass, Castlecomer, Freshford and Kilkenny belonged to the Carlo circuit. When we take into consideration how much work was required to supply all these places, and remember that the preacher lived fourteen or fifteen miles from Mr. Gundy, we will readily see that he could render very little assistance in the erection of the church referred to. It was a great undertaking for him, and shows not only his love for Methodism, but his desire for the spread of the knowledge of Jesus. One important thought connected with the location of the house of God is, that in after years we may be able to regard it as our spiritual home. This sweet word *home* is made more dear and sacred by association with the spiritual interests of the soul, and by the close relation and familiar intercourse of the members of the family of Heaven. This pleasure Mr. Gundy was not to realize at Castlecomer. He had built a house for others, and his comfort must be derived from the satisfaction of having helped them to an advantage which he was compelled to forego. In the midst of all his care and labor to get this place up, and free from debt, he did not forget to attend faithfully his preaching appointments on the Sabbath. He was constant in his duty of preaching the Gospel in the surrounding villages. Cooen, Coolbon,

Girteen and Coolcullen were often the scenes of his acceptable and useful toil, and in these places he formed many warm and familiar acquaintances with the people. In after years he often spoke of these places, and the pleasant hours he spent in intercourse with the many friends he had formed while in the performance of his religious duties. He frequently referred to the happy hours spent in the neighbourhood of Cooen. There lived at that place a school teacher by the name of William Poole. He was a warm friend to Mr. Gundy, and many happy hours they spent in each other's society at Mr. Poole's house. His sons, who were mere lads then, have since grown up to men ; and, their father afterwards emigrating to Canada, they have been for a number of years in important employments in various parts of this country. One of them—the Rev. W. H. Poole, of the John Street Wesleyan Church, Hamilton—has since risen to a very honourable position in the Wesleyan Methodist Church in this Province. Mr. Poole, the senior, was a good scholar, and perhaps was rarely, if ever, excelled in his day, as a school teacher. He was for many, many years the teacher at Cooen, and would, probably, have remained in that position until nature itself had released him ; but, unfortunately for himself, he was a Methodist and was too true to his attachments to deny the fact, and too honest to hide it. He and Mr. Gundy were kindred spirits, and, as their opportunities of converse multiplied, there grew a firm friendship between them, which became the source of mutual joy, and the occasion of many hours of happy intercourse. These good times, long since passed away, were, no doubt, some months ago, renewed in the land where the joy is brighter and the fellowship of all kindred souls is uninfluenced by sin. They now can talk of scenes passed long ago, and can realize to the full the advantages of worship with no fear of disturbance from influential landholders and bigoted churchmen on the one hand, or the Roman Catholic rabble on the other.

In that land, I apprehend, these earthly distinctions are forgotten ; and if a man reaches that glorious country through faith in the Atonement, he is never asked if he were Methodist, Churchman, Dissenter, or Roman Catholic. Nor can it interfere with the joy and communion of that country, to know that from all of the above, and from more sects than these, or even from none at all, will come some of the innumerable host of exalted worshippers. It is inspiring to think of renewing a pleasant earthly acquaintance, amid such associations. They have met there—William Poole and William Gundy—both having passed a long sojourn on earth, both originally from the beautiful Emerald Isle ; but rising from amidst the surroundings of this new world, by the grace of God, have met in heaven, where they feel none of the infirmities of this life, and know none of its cares.

Mr. Poole's adherence to Methodism, cost him his situation. Mr. Gundy's resulted in the loss of his business at Castlecomer ; but Providence was on their side, and no sooner was one door shut against them, than another opened.

The dark cloud **was** immediately followed by **a** bright one; and thus was **made** up to them the sum of their experience in the stern realities of life. I must not forget to mention a little circumstance often referred to by Mr. Gundy, with emotions of gratitude. As **Mr. Poole's** house was always open for the preachers of **the Gospel,** those, both itinerant and local, were brought to share his hospitality, which was freely given for Christ's sake, and was gratefully received by His servants. Mr. Gundy has often told me that very frequently when he was at Cooen, Mr. Poole used to give him his pony to ride most of the way home, and his son, William Henry, then a small boy, would run out to bring the pony back. This little **circumstance**, my dear father-in-law frequently referred to, even in the latter years of his life; and he took a pleasure in doing so, as if the very mention of the circumstance called up the train of happy reminiscences connected with it. Since having renewed his acquaintance with William Henry, now grown to be a man, and rising in popularity and power as a preacher amongst the Methodists of this country, Mr. Gundy delighted to refer to this incident, as he traced back the honor and success of this son, to the earnest and importunate prayers, and faithful and consistent conduct and example of his father. And he was always grateful for having an early connection **with a** Church which afterwards rose to such magnitude, as a great leading agency in spreading "scriptural holiness **over the** world."

CHAPTER V.

HIS ACQUAINTANCE WITH GIDEON OUSELEY—HEARS DR.
CLARKE PREACH—REMOVAL TO PORTARLINGTON, ETC.

THE early part of Mr. Gundy's religious life was spent amid interesting associations. That movement which began in the revival of pure religion, and led to the formation of a Society within the Church of England, was now becoming a felt power in Britain, and Ireland was not wanting in circumstances and men which were calculated to demonstrate the power of the Gospel.

The power of Methodism was heart power, and, shedding its influence over the character and life of its subjects, it was daily supplying a desideratum which the then established forms of religion had failed to furnish. Men were not led to gaze merely upon a barren system, but their hearts warmed under the divine fervour of a blessed reality. While at Castlecomer, Mr. Gundy renewed his acquaintance with Gideon Ouseley, the intrepid apostle of Methodism in Ireland. He had met him years before when quite a lad, but his own house now becoming a home for the preachers in their rounds, he was often honored with Gideon as his guest. From this time there grew an intimacy between them which was never forgotten. They were often together in public and private service in the Master's vineyard, and were frequently side

by side in the streets, on the market squares, and in
various other places, nobly to set forth the imperishable
excellencies of the Saviour of sinners.   There was an
enthusiasm about Ouseley which was well calculated to
stimulate the youthful Christian to action, in hope of the
glorious crown "which the Lord hath promised to them
that love him." Frequently, when at Mr. Gundy's house,
he would take him by the arm and say, " Come, William,
let us be going;" and off they went to preach Christ to
the perishing.   As is well known at the present day, Mr.
Ouseley was repeatedly the subject of violent attack from
the Roman Catholic party. They hurled stones and every
description of missile at him to silence his voice and end
his days if possible, but he was wonderfully preserved.
He often used no little cunning to defeat the object of
his enemies, and, as was very usual for him, planted himself immediately in front of a window which must necessarily be broken if their deeds of murder were persisted
in, and this little piece of caution invariably saved his
head.

Dr. Adam Clarke was another whose influence was, in
his day, perhaps without a parallel in Methodism. His
literary efforts in some degree exceeded his evangelistic;
yet a firmer friend or abler advocate and defender the
Methodists never had.   Those great men were Mr.
Gundy's contemporaries during the earlier part of his
life. He often referred to them and his acquaintance
with their writings; and he was particularly pleased to
note that they were his own countrymen. This country,

so much agitated by Roman Catholic intolerance and by political intrigue, and the ever restless activity of its people in good or bad, has produced many good men who have been an honor to their nation and race, and who have left their "footprints on the sands of time;" and the savour of their lives is yet fresh in our souls. Mr. Gundy, when on a visit to Dublin about the year 1823, was privileged to hear doctor Clarke preach. He says: "I once heard him preach in Dublin from the text, 'God is a Spirit, and they that worship Him must worship Him in spirit and in truth'—a sermon superior, in every sense of the term." He describes Dr. Clarke as "a man of blooming countenance, full habit, thick-set, and full of the fire and warm-hearted pathos so character-istic of the Irish orator." Mr. Gundy purchased his works at the earliest opportunity, and greatly admired them, as the production of a master-mind prompted in its utterances by a holy heart; notwithstanding, he dissented strongly from his views on the Sonship of Christ.

Of Gideon Ouseley, Mr. Gundy says: "I was intimately acquainted with him. Often, often have I heard him preach, and often I have stood beside him when the enraged Papist mob were throwing stones and brickbats to stay the work of this man of God. His sermons were clear expositions of the sacred text — forcible, eloquent, and often overpowering." The Roman Catholics frequently opposed Mr. Gundy while in the exercise of his duties as local preacher, but it was only in threats;

they never attempted physical violence with him. On the contrary, many of them were personally very friendly. His mild and unobtrusive manner generally had the effect of melting the hard-hearted foe into friendliness. I have heard him relate a somewhat singular circumstance, which will show at least that his appearance was no injury to him while travelling in Papist districts. He said: "On Sabbath mornings, as I passed along to my appointments, the Roman Catholics would often do me honor with the most polite religious obeisance of which they were capable,"—mistaking him, no doubt, for a young sprig of the holy priesthood. One day, while on his way to Dublin, he was followed by a Roman Catholic woman, who passed into the hotel after him and earnestly requested confession ; but he got rid of her as well as he could, and continued his journey.

Mr. Gundy, thus wearing the outward aspect of religion, and being always remarked for his mildness of manner by those who knew him best, could not lend himself to any unworthy work. He was a gentleman in his deportment, and the opposition received from the Papist party was more against his religion, and his earnest efforts to propagate it, than against himself. While the facts above narrated show how he wore the appearance of a clergyman, they remind us of the fearful responsibility of the priests, who are thus keeping in blindness a people whose naturally warm and impulsive nature would have attached them firmly to truth, and made them valiant promoters of good.

Men who could thus openly declare their concern of soul, but whose religious yearnings were crushed beneath the heel of an accursed system of mock worship, were worthy of a better religious training than Roman Catholicism was capable of giving. A warmer-hearted, freer, more whole-souled people than the Irish, in the main, can scarcely be found; but it is impossible for human nature to stand under, and throw off, all the crushing weight of satanic power which lies in this diabolical system called Popery. But for this, Ireland would be this day one of the most desirable places of the British Dominion for residence, and her people amongst the most prosperous and happy.

When preaching in the streets, and other out-door places, Mr. Gundy was as much opposed by the church party as by the Catholics. Those were days when it was necessary to unite zeal and prudence. Neither could be successful alone. ·Blind zeal might have sold the cause of the Master, while prudence, without zeal, might have hushed the preacher into the stillness and ease of home retirement and safety. The reckless daring of Peter's impetuosity would be ruinous; not less so, the fear of hidden, yet loving, disciples. The zeal must burn within with holy ardour, and it must be controlled and regulated by the most powerful of agencies—love to Christ.

> " Let my knowing zeal be joined
> With loving charity."

Mr. Gundy now fixed his mind upon Portarlington, as

his next place of business. It was a beautifully situated town, surrounded by a fine stretch of agricultural country. It lay about thirty miles from Castlecomer, and about fourteen from Tullamore—the scene of his boyhood, the sphere of his apprenticeship and early business life ; and the place where the light of true religion first dawned upon his mind, and the love of Christ filled his heart.

They were now connected with the Tullamore circuit, and were enabled to renew many of their former acquaintances with the people of God, from whom, for about seven years, they had been severed. James Johnston was the preacher on the circuit. The Methodist preachers were then beginning to venture beyond the ordinary sphere of their former movements, and some of them were found bold enough to administer the sacraments to the people. This was sometime about the year, 1829, and James Johnson was amongst the first, in that part of Ireland, to favour the people with this important service. From his hands, Mrs. Gundy and her sister—Rev. James Sterling's wife, received the emblems of the Saviour's "broken body and shed blood," for the first time, outside the Episcopalian Church.

For a short time after the opening up of business at Portarlington, Mr. Gundy kept the shop at Castlecomer, and while he gave his principal attention to the former, his mother and Mrs. Gundy attended to the business at the latter. As they were arranging to leave Castlecomer altogether, they supplied very little goods there, but continued to sell off the remaining stock which, when nearly

E

disposed of, they moved down, and gave all their care to the one place.

For some time they were very successful; but they were not long in finding that a town only five miles off, called **Mt.** Mellick, was by far a better market, and, therefore, offered greater inducements to the general merchant than were given in Portarlington, and they **were** strongly inclined to go to this town, thus promising an increase **of** trade.

They, however, continued five years in Portarlington before moving, as they were determined to give it a fair trial prior to assuming the expense and trouble necessarily involved in the change.

Both of these places became, in after years, with many incidents of their stay in each, fixed **firmly in** their memory. Apart from the sacred religious associations and toil, they were ever remembered as the birthplace of several of their children. There is, perhaps, no incident of our lives so well calculated to fix upon the memory our residence at any place, as the care and interest connected with a growing family. In this respect Castlecomer **was** more deeply impressed on their minds than either Portarlington or Mt. Mellick, for in it five of their children were born, **and** beneath its **soil** two them lie sleeping.

One of these died when nearly four years of age—an interesting, beautiful boy—and the other **at** fourteen months. Although many years have passed since they were committed to the dust, yet how often has parenta

affection started the mind on its backward journey, until
they stood beside the new made graves, and with undiminished love for their children, and unwavering faith
in God, they were constrained to say—

> " Ere sin could blight, or sorrow fade,
>   Death came with friendly care ;
> The opening buds to Heaven conveyed,
>   And bade them blossom there."

At Portarlington, as at Tullamore and Castlecomer, Mr.
Gundy was zealous for the cause of his Master, and lost
no opportunity, whether in business hours or not, to drop
a word in season for Him to whom he owed his all. Here
the preachers found him out, and his house was their
home, to which they were ever welcome. During these
times there was kept up in those parts of Ireland a constant
state of agitation between different parties amongst the
Papists. They could agree to persecute and afflict the
Protestants, but could not agree to live peaceably amongst
themselves, and the market-place of Portarlington, near
which Mr. Gundy lived, was the scene of many a great
row between them. They frequently had many a fierce
fight on market days, in which material controversy they
were alternately conquerors and conquered. In all Mr.
Gundy's intercourse with them, although a staunch and
avowed Protestant, yet he never became the object of their
heaviest hatred. This could not arise from any fear or
failure on his part to preach, both in public and private,
those doctrines which aim at the very overthrow of the
Popish system. I can only account for it from the fact of

the unoffending way he had of presenting the truth. I have never yet been able to see the wisdom of those who make a great boast of fearless honesty, while they drive away with all vengeance against those who may differ from them. And, likewise, those preachers, who have an abrupt and daring way of exposing popular sins, might often have been saved a great amount of trouble, and have been far more successful in their object, if the harsh language and angry manner had been wanting, However, it cannot be thus with every man. There are diversities of gifts, and they are all needed, in order to meet the peculiar necessities of this dissolute and sinful world. Perhaps it is, therefore, better not to condemn a man for his manner, if the principle be right, or not contrary to right, so long as the desirable result is gained. There were sons of thunder in the early days, and there were also sons of consolation, and both were necessary and useful.

For several years there was one particular subject before the mind of Mr. Gundy, which gave him much care, and that was the conversion of his mother. She was as yet a stranger to the inward and unspeakable joy produced by a change of heart. A son could scarcely love a mother more than he did; and, as the years wore away, he became increasingly anxious that she should " taste, and know that the Lord is gracious." He often conversed with her on the subject, and frequently, when his concern appeared greater than usual, she would say, " Why, William, do you think I am the worst woman in the world, that you talk so?—sure, I never murdered anyone ;" and thus she continued to show more and more that she did not fully understand the true ground of hope in God. A very commendable course of conduct was continued by Mr. Gundy in the interest he took in the financial state of the churches. In addition to the work of building the church at Castlecomer, he made every possible effort to remove a debt of one hundred pounds which had been incurred in the purchase of a church at Portarlington.

The little band of Methodists had been for years worshipping in a small house in one of the back streets of the town; and when, through his influence, they purchased a very good and commodious building, I think from the Congregationalists, he was fully resolved not to allow the matter to rest until they were free from embarrassment. He here left his business in Mrs. Gundy's hands, and undertook to travel for miles around, amongst the friends of the cause, in order to raise the money, and was, after much toil and care, successful, and had the satisfaction of handing over the amount required to the trustees. This at once removed a great load from the shoulders of the few church-members there, and left them the freer to contribute to the comfort of the travelling preachers, and also to throw themselves afresh into the general work of the Lord. Here, their hard toil together, and the few years of fellowship spent in each other's society, had greatly endeared them to the little church ; and it was with no small degree of reluctance, they gathered up their effects and left for Mt. Mellick.

After moving to this place, they were much pleased to
find a very good Methodist church there.   The Methodists had a standing in Mount Mellick, for a number
of years, and their church was built in Wesley's day.
They were not allowed, however, to hold service during
church hours, although the probability **is, there** were far
more people in the place than could find room in the
parish church.   In this place, as in hundreds of other
towns and villages **in** Britain, the Methodists were determined to hold to Wesley's rule, no matter how **much**
the inconvenience to themselves or the loss to the people.

About this time, a resolution passed the conference,
permitting them to hold service at such times as were
most convenient for themselves, the matter to be decided
by a two-third vote of the quarterly meeting.

The society at Mt. Mellick was determined to have
service in the morning, which seemed the most convenient hour for them; and the matter was shortly to come ·
before the quarterly conference, for the sanction of the
people, according to rule.   The preachers on the circuit,
were Robert Jessop and William Cather.   Jessop favoured,
but Cather as strongly opposed **the** measure, and after a
hard contest, it was carried, much to the improvement of
the congregation and the interests of the society.   From
that time they began to prosper amazingly.   They now
stood on more independent ground, and felt themselves
free to give full scope to their philanthropic and benevo-
lent desires.   During the year 1839, the preachers—Jes-

sop and Cather—were engaged in a gracious revival at
Tullamore, and after the special services were closed
there, they resumed them at Mt. Mellick, with similar
results. The whole church was greatly quickened, and
many young men, who were afterwards useful as preachers and office-bearers, were converted. In this revival,
Mr. Gundy took a prominent part, and all the members
received such a glorious baptism from above as made
them increasingly useful and happy. Mrs. Gundy says
that in that meeting she received such measures of grace
as prepared her for many years of trial, through which
she had afterwards to pass. Mr. Jessop, in a letter to
Mr. Gundy several years after, refers to this work of grace.
His own words will be found on another page of this book.

Their success, added to an inherent feeling of opposition, led the church minister to attack them with great
violence. He lost no opportunity to vent his spleen, and
throw out his heaviest charges against them. He was
not content to do what he could in his private intercourse
with the people, but he made the pulpit the scene of many
a violent dash ; and, by slanderous statement uttered with
vehement gesture, made himself troublesome to the Methodists, and a source of annoyance to the more thoughtful and
less bigoted of his own people. One Sabbath, Mr. Gundy
and Thomas Atkinson—a leading Methodist, and one of
the principal merchants of the place—went to the church,
and it was soon evident to them that this gentleman was
bent on giving the Methodists a heavy blow. He openly
declared, and without any qualification of terms, that both

Fletcher and Wesley were then burning in hell; and, as
he warmed with his theme, he grew furious, and said he
had drawn his sword, and would not sheath it again
until he had thrust it into the very heart of Methodism.
By this wholesale and vulgar attack, he either overshot
the mark, or his missiles fell harmless at the feet of those
he so much hated.   Neither his enmity, fully developed,
nor the malignant hatred of the Papacy, could prevent
this little church, with an open Bible, from succeeding.
Like the Hebrew children they were often in the furnace,
but the "smell of fire was not on them;" they were often
in the lion's den, but the angel of the Lord stood by, and
they were unharmed.   This spirit of oppression, manifested throughout Britain against the Methodists by both
Churchmen and Roman Catholics, can only be understood on the supposition that these parties knew little, if
anything, of the love of Christ shed abroad in the heart.

It is no pleasure to me thus to record the conduct of
these parties, but in giving a faithful history of one who
was so frequently the subject of their hostility, it is impossible to pass it over in silence.

I am forced to show that the progress of Methodism as a
body, or of any of her sons in particular at that time, was
made in the face of the strongest counter-influence, and
therefore proves that in those men of former times there
was a good degree of the true spirit of a disciple of Jesus.
They *denied themselves* and *took up their cross* to follow
Him.   Noble lesson this, and valuable legacy left to us,
their successors.   May we prove ourselves worthy of both.

A few years after going to Mt. Mellick, the potato crop, the chief article of food amongst the poorer classes of the Irish, began to fail, and grim want was already at many a door. This was soon followed by an almost total suspension of business, and nearly every merchant in the country felt the terrible pressure, and most of them were compelled to succumb to the inexorable consequences. During this time they often kept the shop a whole day without taking in more than a half-penny. The only business of any consequence was done on market days, and then one shop would have answered for the whole place. This state of things presented a melancholy contrast with the success they enjoyed on first coming to the place, and they were not prepared for it. For several years this state of things continued without any change for the better, but many for the worse. Each year brought a repetition of the potato rot, which was accompanied with failure amongst the farming community, and the prospects of mercantile men grew darker as the time passed.

CHAPTER VI.

HIS MOTHER'S DEATH—FAILURE IN BUSINESS—COMES TO
NEW YORK—TESTIMONIALS FROM HOME—GOES TO
PITTSBURGH, IN PENNSYLVANIA.

NDER the subduing and sanctifying influences
of religion, the domestic affections are brought
to their highest state of perfection. In illus-
tration of this idea, how great is the contrast between
the untutored savage and the cultivated Christian, in the
interest taken in the comfort and general welfare of aged
parents. While, in the one case, they are heartlessly left
behind the wandering company to die of exposure and
want ; in the other, they are cared for with all the attention
which filial affection can devise. It is true St. Paul says,
"The children ought not to lay up for the parents, but
the parents for the children;" yet this doubtless referred
to the parents during their vigorous manhood, and while
the children were yet in their helplessness ; while, to the
adult child the language of Jesus from the Cross is given
in all the tender solicitude of one who has felt the
promptings of the human breast — "*Son, behold thy
mother.*" Mr. Gundy had now quite a large and interesting family growing up around him. His mother
was also still living with them, and was becoming every
year the object of increasing care ; and although she was
always with him and his family, and had seen real inward

religion illustrated in him, as also in his devoted and pious wife, yet she was still resting in her own natural goodness rather than in the merits of her Redeemer. About four months before her death, and while she was in her usual good health, she was led to "behold the Lamb of God" by faith, and being instructed to venture her all on Him, she was changed from nature to grace. And oh, what a change! "Oh!" she said, "how can it be possible I never saw it in this light before?" She became wonderfully happy, yet not more so than her anxious and now overjoyed son. His highest wish was now crowned, his lifelong prayer answered, and there seemed nothing wanting to make up the sum of his earthly happiness. His mother's days were now spent in praise and prayer. The eyes of her understanding were opened to behold wondrous things in God's law, and she could now see the wisdom of his anxiety for her salvation.

About three months after her conversion she began to show evident signs of approaching dissolution. She grew quite imbecile and, like a little child, would play with the children. On the Sunday evening before her death, she took tea with the family as usual, and walked to bed without assistance. About two o'clock in the morning she called the family and complained of a pain at her heart, and continued about the same throughout the following day.

Anticipating no immediate danger, Mr. Gundy had gone to the prayer meeting on Monday evening, when

suddenly she **was taken** worse. **He was** immediately
sent for, and arrived just in time to see her breathe her
last. She was ninety-five years old when she died. Her
mortal remains were interred in a beautiful little cemetery
about four miles from Tullamore. The Rev. Robert
Jessop, one of Mr. Gundy's most intimate and highly
esteemed friends, conducted the funeral services. Thus
terminated the earthly career of a mother as warmly
loved and as devotedly served as was in the power of a
son to render these evidences of filial regard. He
paid the last tribute of affection by seeing her remains
respectably laid in the tomb, and, while in dissolving
these earthly ties, he was compelled to weep; yet he
rejoiced beyond measure, that she had only gone
before him to heaven, and would await his coming.
His grief at parting would have been much more
intense, if she had been called away before she became the subject of **the** great change of heart before
referred to. He had often contemplated emigrating to
Canada, which was growing in importance every year, as
a British colony, and to which hundreds of his countrymen were going every season; but he could never see his
way clear to do so, while charged with the care of his
aged mother. This difficulty was now removed, and it
was evident that his business must be abandoned on account of the stagnation of trade. The wholesale houses,
perhaps foreseeing the approaching calamity, and wishing to save themselves by disposing of their goods, almost forced the smaller merchants to take a stock larger

than they really needed during this depressed state of business.

After some time, it became clear that a failure must come, and without waiting to fill his own pockets, or in any way enrich his friends, he made an assignment to his creditors and left for this country. After reaching this western world, he sent back a beautifully bound copy of Clarke's Commentary, to be appropriated as would best serve those who had taken possession of his **goods.**

He did not even retain enough money to bring himself and family to this country, but was furnished with an amount sufficient for that purpose, through the kindness of his landlord—James Pim.

He had no correspondence with his **creditors** afterwards, and there is every probability that so general was the bankruptcy of those fearful times for Ireland, that it was beyond the power of any one so to arrange matters as to tell which—the debtor or creditor—the wholesale **or** retail house—or even whether these or the original **pro**ducers, suffered most.

It must be remembered that the circumstances of this failure were altogether unusual, and could, by no means, **be** traced to any want of care or knowledge of business ; much less was it the result of a scheme to enrich himself by unlawful or dishonorable means. I do not wish **to** become **an** apologist for any faults ; nor do I **want to** cover, by numerous words, anything like an unfair proceeding on the part of my deceased father-in-law. If it **were** needed, plenty of proof can be shown that his moral conduct was unimpeachable, and his character untarnished by any act of his at this deplorable time. Letters, from ministers as well as from merchants in Mt. Mellick, commending him for piety, honesty and industry, to both Methodists and merchants of this country, are in my possession, reference to which makes his conduct, in this whole transaction, perfectly justifiable. No man could have foreseen this pressure of business, and few could stand under it when it came. It was a calamity which could not be averted by him, or by the multitudes beside himself, who were compelled to yield to the disastrous results of this terrible Providence. When it was generally known amongst his friends, that he contemplated going at once to America, he was furnished with a number of unsolicited letters, recommending him to friends on this side of the Atlantic. I shall, perhaps, be pardoned if I give a copy of some of these letters, a number of which I have in my possession.

The first here given is from Mr. Joseph Beale, a leading merchant of the place from which he writes, and one who had extensive business connections with the United States. It is addressed to a merchant in New York.

"Mt. Mellick, 3rd mo. 11th, 1842, *Ireland.*

"Jacob Hervey, New York :

"Dear Friend.—This will be presented by William Gundy, who, with his family, removes from this town with the intention of settling in your city. I have known him for some years, and believe him to be an honest and industrious man, and as such, I recommend him to your kind notice, should he have occasion for advice or information in forwarding his intentions as a settler amongst you.

"I remain thine, very sincerely,

"JOSEPH BEALE."

The following will speak for itself:—

"I do hereby certify that Brother and Sister Gundy, of Mount Mellick, have been members of the Methodist Society for upwards of twenty-six years, during which time their profession and conduct have corresponded. They both fear and love God. He has been a leader and local preacher the greater part of that time, much beloved by the Wesleyan ministers and people. Their house has always been open to entertain the messengers of Jesus, and they live in the affections of the people of God. I have been acquainted with them and their family connections during the whole of the above time, and recommend them cordially to the ministers and people of the Methodist Episcopal Church in the United States of America, as a faithful brother and sister in Jesus Christ, our common Lord, hoping they will shew them every mark of Christian love and affection, as they intend shortly to leave their native country to reside in America.

"Given under my hand, this 19th day of January, 1842.

"JOHN ROGERS,
"*Wesleyan Minister*,
"*Mullingar, Longford Circuit.*"

We give one more letter, written by the Rev. Robert
Jessop, Superintendent of the Tullamore circuit, which
embraced the town of Mount Mellick :—" I hereby certify that I have known the bearer, Mr. William Gundy, of
Mount Mellick, for some years.   Long prior to my acquaintance with him, he sustained, **with** credit to himself
and profit to others, the office of local preacher in our
connexion (the Wesleyan Methodist Society).   During the
three years of my superintendency of this circuit (Tulla-
more), Mr. Gundy's conduct has been blameless and irre-
proachable ; and, as far as I was capable of observing and
hearing from others, he adorned the doctrines of God, his
Saviour.   His house has been the home of the preachers,
and his excellent wife stands as high in our estimation for
piety, integrity and uprightness, as himself.   We deeply
regret his loss, and that of his family, to our Zion ; but, as
depression in mercantile life prevails to such an extent at
present in this country, we rejoice that he is about to
unite himself with the large family of the Methodist church
in America.   We commend him and his family to the
grace of God, and to the charge of our brethren, the ministers of the Methodist Episcopal Church of America, and
to the Church herself.

" ROBERT JESSOP,

" Late Superintendent of the Tullamore Circuit."

" Mount Mellick, Feb. 28th, 1842."

I might give copies of several others ; but, while
they would be of interest to the family and friends imme-

diately connected, they would not be so, to the same extent, to the general reader. The Revs. George Burrows, Wm. Richey, Richard Phillips, and Wm. Starkley, all furnished letters, breathing a spirit similar to those already given, which show that, while Mr. Gundy was compelled to leave his native land, no blame can be attached to himself or family, or perhaps to any one else. It was one of the effects of a cause over which no man had, or could have, control. The whole country should have bowed, in sack-cloth and ashes, before God, who had visited the people in judgment on account of the prevalence, and as one of the results, of a system of religion which dishonored Him and degraded His cause. This permitted approach of famine spread desolation and death all over the land, and called forth the pity and prayers of the whole civilized world. There are few general readers who have any conception of the extent of that calamity. If Mr. Gundy had remained longer in Ireland, he would only have made matters worse for himself and others, and, by the complete wasting of his small means, have prevented his escape from inevitable ruin. Five years after they left the shores of their native country, the famine rose to its height.

Dr. Dill, in his eloquently written work on "Ireland's miseries, their cause and cure," thus speaks of the famine in 1847 :—" During the horrors of 1847, our country was transformed into a grave-yard and a lazar-house. It was quite common to see the people staggering like drunken men along the roads from the utter exhaustion of nature, their faces and legs being swollen with hunger;

F

and pages might be filled with the bare record of cases
the most affecting of starvation, pestilence and death.
Let me just present the reader with an instance or two :—
At Killalla, the famished creatures used to crowd around
the house of the Rev. Mr. Rogers, wolfish with hunger ;
and men, once athletic and muscular, would stand before
his windows, take the skin which once covered a brawny
arm, but now hung loose and wrinkled, and double it
round the bone in order to prove the extent of their
emaciation ! One woman was found stretched on the
bed by the side of her dead husband, and after having
just given birth to a poor wasted infant. It was not un-
common to find whole families dead in their cabins together. Nor were the cases rare in which the famished
creatures became deranged before expiring, and in one
such instance—the most awful of all consequences pre-
dicted against the Jews, was found to have taken place—
the delirious mother fed on her dead infant. Our missionaries were doomed to witness daily the most heart-
rending scenes. The Rev. Mr. Brannigan one day
observed a man and his wife digging in a stubble field.
He approached and enquired what they were doing.
They told him they had five children whom they had for
a fortnight supported on cabbage and mill dust, but they
were now actually starving; that for the last two days they
had kept them in bed to try and sleep off the hunger ;
and that they had that day been out from early morning
in quest of some wild roots, of which they exhibited a
handful as the fruits of their protracted labours. Mr.

Brannigan was moved, and, uttering some kind words, he handed them two shillings. This relief coming so unexpectedly on the poor man, weakened as he was by sorrow and hunger, completely unmanned him, and he sobbed and wept in the minister's face; while his wife, still less able to control her feelings, clasped her husband in her arms, exclaiming, 'My dear! our children won't die yet!' And yet these are mere samples. How many scenes more tragic still were enacted during that dreadful calamity, which no chronicle has ever recorded, of whose existence the world never heard, and over which no tears of sympathy were shed, except, perhaps, from some fellow sufferer!"

This state of things was beginning to appear before Mr. Gundy left Ireland. Mrs. Gundy informs me, that on one occasion in particular, a poor emaciated creature came into the shop one day, almost too weak to walk. She would have fallen on the floor but for the timely assistance of those in the place, who not only helped her to a seat, but gave her wine and biscuit, by which she was revived. Such cases were beginning to appear and they were the result of sheer want.— Surely it was a merciful Providence that opened up their way to this land of plenty; for, in Ireland, there was no room for their business, or even the successful prosecution of any other. Hard as it was for them to leave *their own land*, and the many true friends there, it became a matter of necessity. It was with them, either to remain and pass through the awful suffering of the famine, or

move forward to a more plentiful country. In the name
of their God, therefore, and followed by the prayers and
good wishes of numerous friends, they turned their faces
towards the new world; and after the weary sea voyage
of six weeks, in the noble old ship, "George Washing-
ton," they landed in New York on the fourteenth day
of May, 1842, all safe and sound, after the usual eventu-
alities of such a voyage ; and, thankful to God for His preserving mercy, they were buoyant with hope for the future.
It was his intention, when he left Ireland, to remain in
New York ; but he was not long in perceiving that there
was little there in any way congenial to him as a loyal
subject of the British nation. The statements of hatred
towards England, to which he was daily compelled to listen, and the fact that it was difficult to obtain employment there, soon settled his mind to move forward to
find some spot, if possible, more congenial to his tastes,
and more inviting as a place of business.

While in New York, he made his way to the Methodist
book-room, and presented his papers to a number of the
ministers who were gathered there, amongst whom was
the Rev. John Ryerson, from Canada, who was there on
conference business. Mr. Gundy **was now** fully resolved
to enter the itinerant ministry, if his way was made clear.
These gentlemen were highly pleased with his recommen-
dations ; but, as there were no vacancies just then, they
could not employ him in their work. Being now advised
by one whom he took to be a friend, and whom he considered fully acquainted with the country, he resolved to

go on to Pittsburg, in Pennsylvania. After a very toil-
some and unpleasant journey, they arrived, worn and
weary, at the black, smoky city; but here his way was
darker than ever : for there was no prospect of anything
in the shape of business opening for him. This was a
dark hour for them : for they were all nearly worn out
with the toil of travelling, and, worse than all, their funds
nearly exhausted. They were in a strange land, and were
far from the counsel and assistance of friends ; but their
hope was in God. They had learned, through all their
difficulties in the old world, to trust more fully in God ;
and, though perplexed on every side, they were not in
despair,—though cast down, they were not destroyed.
The trial was indeed great for Mr. Gundy. If he had
been alone, it would not have been half as great ; but the
thought of having his partner and seven children, most of
whom were helpless, depending upon him, very much increased his perplexity and uneasiness of mind. His way
seemed entirely hedged up ; but, encouraged by his heroic
and ever faithful wife, he started alone for Canada, where
he hoped to find, on British soil, a settled home for himself and family.

CHAPTER VII.

HIS LANDING IN CANADA—EMPLOYMENT IN TORONTO—
ENTERS THE ITINERANT MINISTRY, ETC.

THERE comes an hour in the trials of most men when their sorrows reach the fulness of darkness and discouragement, and then gradually recede. Happy is it for mortals that we are not altogether dependent upon the ordinary prescience of men. Hopeful as the mind **may** be in its natural construction, we can see but a very short distance before us in life. When the clouds and mists, accumulating for years, so far increase in density as to obscure the light of the sun ; deserted of man, and failing of friendly aid from any earthly quarter ; it is pleasant and cheering indeed to be able to close the eyes upon a stormy world, and by faith perceive the nearness and preciousness of the Father above. To hear, amidst the noise and commotion of the stormy elements, the one familiar voice, in accents of love, saying,—

> " I'll be with thee, I'll be with thee,
> Only *all* my counsel take.
> I will never, never leave thee,
> I will *never thee* forsake."

This is **one boast** of our religion. The roaring of the storm can never be so loud as to drown the Father's voice; the cloud never so dark as to hide the Saviour's **face ;** and the trial never so severe as to prevent his pity.

So did Mr. Gundy and his partner find the consolations of religion when they most needed them. They always found a welcome at the throne of grace, and always retired from the mercy seat under the inspiring voice of the Master, " My grace is sufficient for thee."

Mr. Gundy was not long in reaching Canada, and was glad of heart to place his foot on British soil once more. He landed in Toronto in the month of June, 1842, only a month or so after coming to New York. Here he met with several friends from Ireland, and by the assistance of one John Phillips, with whom he was acquainted in the old country, he obtained a situation as salesman in the establishment of Mr. Porter, then doing a good business in the dry goods line.

In a short time he sent for his family, and in the month of August—nearly two months after he came—he had the satisfaction of seeing them around him, with better prospects for the future than they had known since before the decline of trade in Ireland. Mr. Gundy was a man of careful business habits, and from the ever multiplying and pressing wants of a numerous family, it was necessary, not only to be dilligent, but economical ; and urgent as were these claims and those of his business at Mr. Porter's store, he never lost sight of his duty to his heavenly Father, and was ever ready for an opportunity to be of service in His cause. He, therefore, soon found out the Methodist church and the Methodist preachers.

After presenting his papers from the Irish preachers, he was soon employed at his much loved labor in the

vine-yard of the Lord. He was at once at work in the
pulpit, in the capacity of a local preacher, and was nearly
every Sabbath away somewhere, holding forth the word
of life to the people. The townships around Toronto,
were the scenes of his first efforts in this country. He
travelled into various parts of Whitchurch, York, Toronto
township, and along the Kingston road, both east and
west from Toronto. He related rather an amusing incident of an early adventure he had in Canadian woods
and roads, during his first winter.

He had been out assisting the Rev. Mr. Dandy, in
holding a meeting in Whitchurch on the Sabbath morning. He got along very well on his way out, but unfortunately for himself, he yielded to the earnest request of
Mr. Dandy, and remained to preach for him in the evening ; after which service, he had to drive back to the city
in order to be ready for his work in the morning.

He was not long in travelling towards home, when he
lost his way; and seeing a light in the distance, he made,
as best he could, for the house ; and, to his enquiry after
the road to Toronto, the woman replied by telling him to
go straight through the *bush* until he came to the road.
He did not know what in the world she could mean by
the bush; but without asking her to explain these Canadian
terms, he allowed the horse to go much as he was inclined,
and after several fruitless enquiries, he found himself prevented, only by a fence, from rushing headlong into the
small lake on Yonge street, several miles from Toronto.

After moving about hither and thither for some time,

he met a man who gave him fresh instructions; and after upsetting the cutter and finding himself under it, with the alternative either to lie there until morning or to dig himself out, and after resorting to the latter plan, and being the subject of a few more difficulties, he found himself nearing home at daylight in the morning. This was his first real adventure in driving along Canadian roads in a Canadian winter, and certainly he had no very strong inclination for a repetition of the scenes. On the contrary, he was grateful to God for His preserving mercy, and was fully resolved to make his journeys in the future as much as possible by daylight, a rule which it is well known could not be long kept after he had entered the itinerant ranks. But, becoming more accustomed to these roads and to the management of a horse, he had less difficulty than on this night, long to be remembered by him.

To show that the uppermost concern with him was to do good, and that his mind led him especially to the work of preaching Christ, we may remind our readers that, during his darkest hours in New York and Pennsylvania, he was active in preaching Jesus to the people; and this he was always willing to do, according to the usual and orderly arrangements of the Methodist Church. Instead of making an appointment on his own responsibility, he procured a license from the proper authorities, and then set forward to further the plans and promote the objects of the regular work of the Church. His license, signed by Wilson Bleakey, Secretary, and W. C. Henderson,

Presiding Elder, is dated 10th of June, 1842, or a little over three weeks from the time of coming to the country, and shows that, even though a stranger and then unsettled, and greatly perplexed to know what course to take in order to secure a home for himself and family, he was not by any means willing to allow the time to pass unimproved.

How much better it would be for all church members, in moving from one place to another, to remember that a large measure of their own happiness, and the fact of their usefulness to others, depends a great deal on whether or not they at once become connected with the Church of Christ in the vicinity of their new home. A person may go forward in a sphere of usefulness, or he may grow careless and become lukewarm, or may fall from grace altogether, as he either joins, or neglects to join, with the people of God in those religious exercises which contribute so much to the general good of God's children.

If from this personal interest in the matter we were all to act, the Church and we ourselves would be all the better for it. No man who is a Christian should be ashamed of his profession ; and instead of depending, as a weak and helpless child, upon the presence of some guardian angel, or expecting, perchance, to be found and carefully guarded by some ever-watchful member of the Church, he should stand erect with mingled feelings of holy pride and joy, that he is accounted worthy of a name and a place amongst the people of God.

Mr. Gundy was employed in the store of Mr. Porter

only about one year, preaching, as I have said, in all the country round about, as well as frequently in the city, when Dr. Richey—the chairman of the district—urged him to commit himself fully to the work of the ministry. His mind had been for a long time leading him in this direction, and he was evidently awaiting quietly the events of Divine Providence which might open up his way to this much desired work. It cannot, however, be said that any but the purest of motives could have prompted him to follow the advice, or obey the *command*, of Dr. Richey. It was a course which would require much self-denial, and would entail many trials. After-experiences proved this to be too true ; but in committing himself fully to the Lord he was prepared for the one, and in the energy and patience of a faithful soldier he could endure the other. Some time during the summer of 1843 he was sent to the Markham circuit. He evidently entered upon the work with the full impression that he was guided by his heavenly Father ; and, as it regards his call to preach, his mind was quite settled, and had been for several years. He was waiting with the prayer on his lips, "Here am I—send me ;" and now that the command was given, "Son, go work to-day in my vineyard," he obeyed and went.

He was by no means disposed to "think more highly of himself than he ought to think" ; and, if I have any correct idea of his motives, his strongest desire was to glorify God, and be made useful in saving souls. There was a circumstance which took place at this time, and which added very much to the measure of his happiness, and that was the appointment of his eldest son, John, to a circuit in the same body, and sent out by the same authority. Dr. Richey had been holding meetings in the neighborhood where John was teaching school, in the township of Whitchurch, and was staying at the house where he boarded; and one morning, after asking John a number of questions in history, theology, &c., &c., gave him to understand that he wished him to enter the ranks of the Christian ministry, which he did, and was soon engaged in a work of extensive usefulness.

It was a source of great joy to Mr. Gundy, as well as to his devoted wife, to see their children, in early life, finding the Saviour. But that joy was much increased when their eldest son—their first-born—was giving promise of usefulness, and was, simultaneous with his father, to enter, with the unreserved consecration of their powers of body and soul, into the highest and noblest employment which can in any way engage the attention or enlist the sympathies of man. John was quite young, and gave fair promise of making a man of considerable pulpit ability. He was sent to Brantford, as his first circuit.

Mr. Gundy remained one year on the Markham circuit, when the district meeting, which was the highest council of this branch of Methodism in Canada, gave him his next appointment to the Pickering circuit, where he remained for two years. I may remind my readers that the only Methodist bodies in this Province, at that time, of which he had any extensive knowledge, were those known as the British Wesleyans, under the superintendency of Dr. Richey, and the Canadian body, commonly known as the Ryerson Methodists. The Canadian Wesleyans, formed by Elders Ryan and Jackson, were comparatively unknown to him then, although they had an existence since 1829; and, besides this, the English Methodist New Connexion missionary, Rev. John Addyman, had landed on our shores about six years before, and the union between the denomination which he was forming and the above-named Canadian Wesleyans was, a few years prior to the time of which we write, completed, and at that time this body was assuming considerable proportions.

He had not, as yet, been made acquainted with the peculiarities of their polity, and had, perhaps, heard of them only as the much despised Kilhamites. Providence had cast his lot amongst the Wesleyan Methodists; and he was willing to give his energies to the work of promoting their interests. During his stay at Markham and Pickering, he was greatly encouraged with good and increasing congregations. There were no very extensive revivals at this time, of which we can give any account, but the work in his hands seemed to grow steadily nevertheless. During his stay on the Pickering circuit, he found the sect known as Millerites, greatly agitating the people with their pre-millenarian views. The whole country was inflamed to a wonderful degree of excitement on account of the declared speedy coming of the Son of Man to set up his kingdom, and begin his thousand years' reign on the earth. Mr. Gundy had often to combat their unscriptural and pernicious doctrines. This he felt it his duty to do on several occasions ; but at one particular time, when these prophetical pretenders had been unusually troublesome, he was induced to preach especially to meet their oft repeated statement relative to the improbabilities that when Christ came he would destroy the material heavens, and close up his mediatorial kingdom. He first entered into the scriptural evidences of the coming of Christ, not to reign bodily, but to appear in judgment ; and then by skilfully arranging a philosophical argument—by explaining the chemical composition of the atmosphere—showed how very easy a thing it would be for the great Creator, by the passage of an electric current through the oxygenized air, to fire as in a flash all the world, changing the very water into sheets of flame, and, as with the besom of destruction, sweeping away all living things from off the earth. He thus became as troublesome to these Millerites as they were to the Christians ; and while he successfully neutralized *their* teachings, he comforted the hearts of *his* people with the cheering doctrines of the cross. He had a very clear view of scripture doctrine in his best days ; and, in earnestly holding forth the word of life, his own soul was comforted while he gave encouragement to others. From Pickering, he received his next appointment to the Brock Circuit in 1846. At that time the township of Brock, as almost all that section of country, was a comparative wilderness. The roads were mere passes through the bush, in many places almost impassable during several months of the year. It was impossible to use a buggy and make the speed necessary to enable a minister of the gospel to get from one appointment to another in the allotted time. In many places streams had to be forded ; and, what was often more difficult and attended with greater danger, many of the swamps had to be forded also. Some of them were bridged by laying down parallel logs, but these, without a covering of earth, were both unpleasant and unsafe. This was a new order of things to him. He had lived all his life thus far **amidst** the many material advantages of an old country ; and, now to go from the few improvements which the frontier settlements of this land presented to where there was almost everything of the backwoods life to contend with, was more than he anticipated when he left his native land. But having given himself to the Master's work, it was not in him to choose the sphere of his labours, and he entered upon the duties of this new field with a heart trusting in God for the success he so much desired.

Michael Wilson, a member of his last circuit, and who was the son of Mr. Gundy's old friend, and first employer in Ireland, went with his team to move them out to their new home. The journey was somewhat lengthy and tedious. They could not accomplish it in one day, and night overtook them at a place familiarly known as the "long woods," some where near the village of Uxbridge. Here they found shelter and comfortable lodgings in the house of a Roman Catholic family, who were exceedingly kind to them, as most of the new settlers were, especially to strangers. It is much to be feared **that the successors**

of these hardy sons of toil do not possess this spirit to the
same extent. Then they knew how to sympathize with
each other, for they were nearly all strangers alike to each
other, and the new country which they had adopted as
their own. However this may be, in the morning our
travellers, much refreshed in body, resumed their journey,
and reached the parsonage during the day—and such a
parsonage! Just think of it, a small log house in the
midst of an almost impenetrable forest, approached by
the road along which they had come—and oh, what a
road! Think of this my brethren of the itinerancy.
We aspire to better parsonages and circuits, but such as
these our fathers endured in hope of leaving us better
provided for. When they came to this place, destined to
be for three or four years their home, they found some provisions left for them by the Rev. Samuel Fear, Mr. Gundy's
predecessor. In blissful ignorance of the fact that they
were possessed of a beautiful well of never failing water,
they made tea from the soft water, and thought themselves happy to be possessed of that same. They brought
a new milch cow and a number of hens, and thus began
their entrance upon a work which afterwards proved a
source of encouragement to them, and of great spiritual
advantage to many who are yet living.

They were not long in forming an acquaintance with
the people of their charge; the most of whom, from their
loyalty to the laws of the land, had connected themselves
with the cause of the British missionaries. The Ways,
Harts, Jacksons, and many others, he often spoke of

until within a short time of his death, with many tender reminiscences of the happy times he spent amongst them. He was on their circuit but one year when the union took place between the Ryerson party and the British conference, which union was formed in the year 1847.

He was returned as one of the ministers of the united body for two years more—viz., 1847 and 1848—and this was a happy circumstance for the people of that circuit, who were so intensely British in their feelings that they would not receive a minister who had formerly belonged to the Canadian Methodists. Whether they regarded them as disloyal to British rule, or what was the exact nature of their objections, we cannot say ; but they had previously fully resolved that if the union were carried, they would have only those who were formerly British missionaries to be their ministers. When Mr. Gundy returned to Brock after the union, there was no little excitement amongst the Methodists. He found nearly the whole community in arms against the conference, and so far was this spirit carried, that those who were British Methodists refused to allow the conference preacher to occupy the churches which they themselves had built, and which they were resolved should be appropriated to their own use, and consequently they closed them, only to be opened to whomsoever they would. The churches were closed against Mr. Gilbert the conference preacher, and, although Mr. Gundy was as yet, under the conference, as the assistant preacher to Mr. Gilbert, the people were ready to hear him and give him every

G

possible attention.   Providence Chapel, not far from the
residence of George St. John, was closed, and one
beautiful Sabbath morning, as Mr. Gundy went to his
appointment there, he found the church locked, and the
people gathered in crowds around the door.   They at
once said they would open it for him but not for his
superintendent; but he being a lover of order, and
withal wishing to bring the people to submit to the
conference arrangement and manifest true loyalty to the
church, refused to go in.   In a short time some one of
their number effected an entrance by the window and
opened the door, and at once a general rush was made
for the church, the crowd carrying Mr. Gundy along with
it, who, being thus forced to do that from which his
feelings naturally shrank, and not liking at all the spirit of
insubordination manifested, arose and commenced the service by announcing the hymn beginning—

> " Into a world of rebels sent,
> I walk on hostile ground,
> Where impious men, on ruin bent,
> And hellish hosts abound."

The service passed without any other circumstance of
a very serious nature, save that he labored hard to show to
the people Jesus Christ as a present Saviour—one whom
too many of them had rejected and injured, but who **was**
even then "waiting to be gracious."

CHAPTER VIII.

ATTENDS CONFERENCE IN 1849 — IS REFUSED ORDINA-
TION — LEAVES THE WESLEYANS, AND JOINS THE
NEW CONNEXION.

IT may be said that disappointments are the
common lot of humanity. The existence of
hope, however, will not allow us to anticipate
them, for by *it* we are promised prosperity every day. It
is well for us that the general experience of men tones
down the high-born ambition of *hope*, and often treats ex-
cessive incredulity to a bitter taste of real life. The poetry
of humanity paints the future with golden glories, while
the common prose of life restores the general level of me-
diocrity, and furnishes an atmosphere when the flights of
fancy give place to the plain and practicable. Thus, the
balance of power is preserved by these counter-working
elements, and men are not allowed to feed on ecstacy on
the one hand, or compelled to suffer from dejection or
melancholy on the other. The glorious *illumination* of
the clear sky prepare us for the *dark* cloud and the gathering storm.

In these matters of human experience, no **man is so well**
prepared to make the most of life's profits and enjoyments
as the Christian. He meets his difficulties with fortitude,
and overcomes them in patience. The place of his refuge

is the throne of grace, which is also the source of his strength.

A storm was gathering for Mr. Gundy; but his intercourse with the people of Brock, with his family, and especially with the mercy seat, was preparing him to pass through it in safety. At the conference of 1849, he went up to the annual gathering, fully expecting to be ordained and received into full connexion with the body. But in this he was doomed to disappointment, for, as he was a married man, and somewhat advanced in years, they refused him this privilege. He had travelled six years— three with the British missionaries, and three with the conference after the union,—and it was reasonable that he should expect some other position than merely that of assistant. He now saw, however, very plainly, that he was to be left in the capacity of hired help, doing the principal work of the Lord in the pulpit from Sabbath to Sabbath, and during the days of the week, but was to be denied the privilege of a proper ministerial standing amongst his brethren. He was called to this work by the British missionaries, no doubt, with the understanding that he should receive, at the proper time, the usual orders of ministerial office ; but immediately upon the completion of the union there came into power those who knew him not, and hence the treatment he received. Another trial was now before him. He could not think of remaining where he was, to be kept all his life in an inferior position amongst his brethren, and especially when he had the true Methodistic seal to his ministry—the conversion of souls ;

and also when he remembered that there were others, **in** both intellectual and theological attainments, his inferiors, who were favored with the very thing denied to him. To **leave** them was also a great trial to him, for, from early life, he had always been strongly attached to the Wesleyan Methodist Church, and up to this time he had left nothing undone in **order** to further the objects of that body. His early days were devoted so fully to the work of the Lord amongst them, that he had willingly suffered reproach, shame and loss, and he had diligently toiled to make this church, spiritually and materially, the gainer. Nothing but the positive refusal of the con⁻ ference to accord to him what was fairly his due, and by so doing unnecessarily humiliate him, and deprive him of a place amongst men, for which he had, at least, fair qualifications, could ever have led him to bid them adieu, and force him to seek elsewhere a sphere of usefulness. He now saw that the only course open to him was entirely to sever his relations ; and being previously invited by several influential members of the New Connexion in Toronto and elsewhere, and having care-fully considered the matter, and committing himself fully into the hands of Providence, he resolved to unite with the last named church, whose conference was then sitting in Cavan, near Port Hope. As soon as it became known, **that** he thought seriously of taking this step, Dr. Richey, and other of his personal friends, came to him and did all in their power to induce him to remain until the next conference, and **they would** pledge themselves to have

fairness dealt out to him, in the matter. From **the reasons** above stated, which he thought sufficient, his mind
was fully set to leave the conference ; and besides this,
he evidently saw, that, had the laity, who knew him, any
voice in the matter, he would have been differently dealt
with. So, after presenting his resignation to those who
had called him into the itinerant work, he, with **as** little
delay as possible, laid his papers before the New Connexion conference, and was accepted, and sent as a missionary to Brock, in which place he had already labored three
years. This step appeared necessary, and was pressed
upon him at that particular time. **His** mind being clear
to move, it must be done before returning home, or perhaps not for another year ; so, without the satisfaction of
a consultation with Mrs. Gundy, for this was impossible,
seeing she was in Brock, and he in Toronto, and many
long miles of weary road lay between them, he applied
and was received and commissioned as above stated. It
was only in an urgent case, that he could be persuaded
to make so important a change as this, without first laying
the whole subject before his much loved partner, for counsel and advice. No man could value the counsels of a
wife, more than he did ; and few were more ready to follow them. In such matters, he was highly favoured, for
Mrs. Gundy was not only ready to help him, but her
good, sound sense, and the practical cast of mind she
had, qualified her to render valuable service. This was
peculiarly necessary in his case, for, in his nature, he was
full of generous sympathy. The promptings of his over-

liberal nature, would often have made him the subject of
severe imposition, if it had not been for.the timely assistance of Mrs. Gundy; and, in all the numberless questions arising from the ordinary business of life, he found
invaluable help from her. These things considered, it
was an unusual circumstance for him to take so important
a step as to leave one church and join another without
first laying the matter before his wife, and then jointly
bending with it before the throne of grace for Divine
counsel and guidance. The first we have shown to be
impossible ; and as for Divine guidance, his course **was**
very clearly marked out for him. One door was closed
by a refusal to ordain and receive him into full connexion,
and another was at once opened where these things could
be received; and, besides, it was only another branch of
the same family—the eldest son of the Methodist mother
—and, withal, promising the advantages of a form **of**
government more congenial to his feelings and scriptural
views.

This latter fact is clearly borne out by statements of
his own made repeatedly upon the public platform and in
the quiet retirement of fireside conversation ; and subsequent events prove this to have been a wise choice.

When Mr. Gundy returned to Brock in 1849, he **was**
not a Wesleyan, but a New Connexion, preacher. **As I**
have said, the greater part of the Methodists of Brock
were strongly attached to the British Methodists, and
were as much opposed to the Canadians ; **and,** when Mr.
Gundy returned, **the most of them** quietly withdrew and

passed over to the New Connexion, and objected to hear the representative of a conference which had refused to him the powers and privileges of ordination.

This was considered by the Brock friends a grievous wrong done to one whom they had learned to love as a faithful pastor and firm friend, and the stroke was felt by them almost as much as by himself.

Mr. Gundy did not find fault with the decision of the conference. It was their own business, and they had a right to carry out their own convictions; but they must bear the consequences of their own action. Of course, in the matter of his leaving, the Wesleyans would sustain no irreparable loss; it was only the loss of one man, and he only six years in the ministry. But this evidently involved the removal of a number of members in Brock, and also resulted in opening a way into the New Connexion for Mr. Gundy's three sons, who have since entered the itinerant ranks. The whole thing, to me, however, looks too much like the unfeeling, high-handed measure of a secular court, to be the deliberate and calm Christian conclusion of an ecclesiastical assembly, whose breasts are supposed to be moved by the feelings of a common brotherhood. If I am not very much mistaken, the conference, subsequent to Mr. Wesley's day, has failed to exhibit the spirit of adaptation which so much distinguished him as "a child of Providence." I know that we are often charged with being dissenters, factious, &c., &c.; yet I am not so sure but the conference of the parent body is responsible for most, if not all, of the divisions in the

Methodist family. At the present day, a calm observer of events, or a close and thoughtful reader of history, can scarcely fail to see, in the origin of the New Connexion, a needful reformation—an advance step—which would have been taken at the time by the whole body but for the over-zealous and purblind spirit of a gigantic conservatism. I have no disposition to interfere with the good feeling which exists between ourselves and our Wesleyan friends ; but it is impossible that, in giving the history of one who was so many years a Wesleyan, and so many a New Connexion, I should fail to notice these facts. The many changes made in the usages of the parent body, and the possession of a liberal spirit, together with the admission of the laity into the Wesleyan conference, may, ere long, result in making Methodism, in Canada, in organic life, as she has always been in doctrines and ordinances, one and inseparable ; and, towards this result, recent movements are showing signs of encouragement. The Lord hasten the time. After the excitement in Brock, caused by the union above referred to, and also by Mr. Gundy's joining the New Connexion, had subsided, he continued the work of his high calling without any material interruption, and he was that year, as during all the former years of his stay in Brock, blessed with a good degree of prosperity.

He often referred with gratitude and joy to a very gracious work, done through his instrumentality, in a Roman Catholic family, who resided several miles from the parsonage. His appointments spread out into Mariposa, and even extended as far as the town of Lindsay.

One of these appointments in Mariposa, on a week night, was held in a tavern, the landlord's wife being a member, and one evening, as Mr. Gundy was preaching, a young man of Roman Catholic parentage was a careful listener. After going home he reported to the family what wonderful things he had heard, and his father, in a short time, made it a point to hear for himself. Mr. Gundy was made aware of the presence of this man when he came, and suited his subject accordingly. The Spirit of Truth applied the Word, and he went home, saying, "If Mr. Gundy is **right** I am wrong, and I shall know for myself." So saying he repaired to the Bible, and his eyes were opened, and in a short time he and his family embraced Christ. He became strongly attached to Jesus, and re-nounced with all his heart the nonsense of the Church of Rome. He died soon after this, happy in the Saviour, and in full expectation of a seat at His right hand. This circumstance was the occasion of great comfort to Mr. Gundy, as he was exceedingly glad to lead the poor deluded devotees of Rome to the Lamb of God. He **was** pleased to hear their words of gratitude, to see the expressions of joy beaming from their countenances, and **to** hear them speak of the glorious prospect which **awaited them** above. This was his life work, and his soul delighted in it.

During part of his time in Brock he had a violent attack of fever and ague, which continued to dis-tress him for three months. About three weeks of this **time he** was confined **to** the house, but during

the remainder he filled his appointments, often shaking
with the chills as he rode along in the saddle from
place to place. He was very much weakened and
reduced in flesh, but through the kindness of his friends,
and the merciful interposition of Providence, he was again
restored, and continued his duties until the close of his
stay on the circuit.

While passing through his numerous labors, and
patiently enduring his affliction, his mind often wandered
back to his native land, and his many friends there. His
labors in the church and in his business all passed frequently in review before him. He was also often cheered
by the receipt of letters from home. Those from his old
friend and pastor, the Rev. Robert Jessop, were specially
welcome, inasmuch as they contained the affectionate
expressions of a true friend. Mr. Jessop was a man of
no ordinary ability. He possessed a fine commanding
appearance, was a scholar of high attainments, rich in the
charms and graces of true eloquence, and withal he was
an earnest Christian and a loving friend. Mr. Gundy
often spoke of the happy hours they spent as fellow-
laborers in the gracious revival with which the church in
Mt. Mellick was visited during 1839 and 40, and of the
sweet Christian intercourse which they enjoyed together
in the family circle, during Mr. Jessop's visits to Mt.
Mellick. Mr. Jessop's letters contained touching allusions to the scenes and associations of the past. He
speaks in one of them as follows :—

"COURTNEY HILL, NEWRY,

"*February 16th*, 1848.

"MY DEAR BROTHER GUNDY,—Your very kind favour of December the 18th, came to hand on the first of this month. We were much gratified by a line from you. It is so refreshing to our spirits to learn that you, Mrs. Gundy, and family are well, and that you are so fully engaged in our common Master's cause. May you be very successful in your divine vocation.

"I **often** call to remembrance, but **more** especially when favoured **by a line from your** pen, the scenes—the glorious scenes—of 1839 and 40, when amid opposition— the well organized opposition—of the enemies of Methodism, we **were** favoured with such **an** outpouring of the Holy Ghost as added hundreds **of** saved souls to our Zion. Some of them now—not less than seven—able ministers of the New Testament; and in addition, many others, useful and efficient church officers, whose services have been greatly owned of God. So we have seen **verified** the testimony of the Psalmist, 'He that sitteth in **the heavens** shall laugh at them.' Your much esteemed letter was not read with unmingled **feelings.** Dear Ellen's* death cast a gloom over our joys. **Her** attention and

---

* This refers to a sister of **Mrs.** Gundy, who came to this country with them. A year or two after coming to Toronto, she was married to a wealthy gentleman, Mr. Thomas Dean. She lived between three and four years after her marriage, and died of fever. She was greatly lamented by the family, who have cherished, and still do, the fondest recollections **of** her amiable disposition and unassuming piety.

solicitude for my comfort, when it was my privilege to be
the occupant of the prophet's chamber in your hospitable
domicile, (only surpassed by dear Mrs. Gundy's never to
be forgotten kindness), will long be remembered ; but
she is gone. Alas ! how uncertain is life ! I had, until
a few months ago, hoped to see you all once more in the
flesh at no very distant period ; but should the good providence of God so order that I shall reach your shores,
the pleasure is denied me, as one is now numbered among
the dead, but I hope also amongst the redeemed of the
Lord, 'who have washed their robes and made them
white in the blood of the Lamb.'"

CHAPTER IX.

ATTENDS THE DISTRICT MEETING IN TORONTO—HIS LA-
BORS IN THE PRINCE EDWARD, CAVAN AND OX-
FORD CIRCUITS.

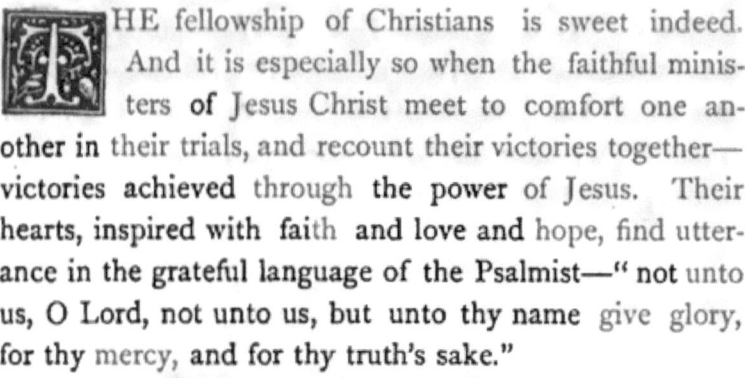THE fellowship of Christians is sweet indeed. And it is especially so when the faithful ministers of Jesus Christ meet to comfort one another in their trials, and recount their victories together—victories achieved through the power of Jesus. Their hearts, inspired with faith and love and hope, find utterance in the grateful language of the Psalmist—" not unto us, O Lord, not unto us, but unto thy name give glory, for thy mercy, and for thy truth's sake."

No one could more appreciate Christian intercourse and fellowship, than Mr. Gundy. It was his delight, after a season of "battling for the Lord," to meet his brethren in the various councils of the Church. He was not formed for the hermit's cell, but his joy was in interchanging his thoughts and blending his sentiments with those of real *live men*, whose hearts were filled with the love of Jesus, and whose ambition was to glory in His cross. In the fall of the year, 1849, he met his brethren in the district meeting in Toronto. I find, in the Methodist New Connexion Magazine for the same year, a report from Rev. H. O. Crofts,—the General Superintendent of Missions in Canada—to the English Conference ;

in which the following, in relation to Mr. Gundy, is given
from the pen of the Rev. Wm. McClure, then chairman
of the Toronto district :

" Brother Gundy is proving himself the right sort of
man—diligent, faithful, and devoted to God ; he has
many pressing invitations from respectable parties to
preach, and from Societies among them ; but his plan is
already full. His circuit will be fully able to raise for
him the salary of a young man, and to make up something handsome for missionary purposes. The district
meeting, therefore, recommends the annual committee
to grant him the other twenty-five pounds, to make up
his salary."

And in another part of the same report, Mr. McClure
says "Mr. Gundy, of whom mention is made, was received
at the last conference, and appointed to a new station,
called Brock ; he has now forty-five members under his
care, and there is every prospect of an increase."

The conference at which he was received, sat in June,
and on the eighth day of the following month, July, he
was ordained for "special purposes." His certificate of
ordination is signed by the following ministers :—William
McClure, Thos. Talbot Howard, and Frederick Haynes.
At the next conference, in June, 1850, he was received
into full connection, and was thus fully prepared to exercise the functions of the holy office. At this conference,
he received an appointment to the Prince Edward circuit, which was situated in the old Prince Edward district, of which Picton is the chief town. On this circuit,

he gave himself to the same earnest toil which had previously engaged his hands, and was similarly rewarded
with success. One feature of his success, which made it
more interesting to him, was the fact that, at one of his
special meetings, four of his own children were hope-
fully converted. The two eldest were brought to God
in Ireland; but, until the time of this meeting, the rest
of them were out of the ark of safety. The fact of his
children being led to Jesus, by his own instrumentality,
was cause of unspeakable joy to him, and gave rise
to frequent expressions of gratitude to God, for His wonderful love.

While in that part of the country, he formed many
happy acquaintances; and, friendships formed with him
were not soon forgotten. There, he met for the first time,
on Canadian soil, the son of his old, long tried and much
esteemed friend, Mr. Poole. This son was no other than
the promising lad, with whom years before, he was intimately acquainted, in his father's home at Cooen. He
had grown to be a man of fine, commanding appearance; was, some years before, received by the Wesleyan
conference, and was now the Wesleyan minister in Picton. Mr. Gundy called upon Mr. Poole there, and renewed his acquaintance with him, and loved him for his
many excellencies of head and heart, but *especially* for
his father's sake.

Mr. Gundy remained on this circuit for two years, and
at the conference of 1852, held in the Bethel chapel, on
the Welland canal circuit, he was appointed to the Cavan

circuit. At that time, Cavan was quite a new township ; at least, it was regarded as amongst the newer settlements of the country, although many of the farms were beginning to show signs of advanced improvement. It was principally settled with Irish, from the county Cavan, Ireland. They were very firm Protestants, and, at that time, so bitter was their hatred to Popery, that they would scarce-
ly allow a Roman Catholic family to reside in any part of the township. Whether it was for the purpose of having an organized force, with which to carry out their hostility to Roman Catholicism, or merely to further their schemes for amusement, I know not, but large numbers of the young men of the country were banded together, and seemed to rule the entire place. They indicated their wants in secresy, and carried out their plans under cover of the night ; and were known as the "Cavan Blazers"—
a lawless banditti—whose conduct was often extremely disgraceful—sometimes magnanimous ; and so powerful were they that no man could be found to complain of them, and no magistrate with sufficient courage to issue a warrant for their arrest. You may say surely there was much need of a gospel minister, who, going in the name of the Divine Master, and in the use of His means, might be instrumental in effecting a moral reformation amongst them. The people of Mr. Gundy's charge, however, were an earnest, kind-hearted, praying people. He found very many to give him a hearty welcome, and, by prayer and otherwise, to help forward the objects of his mission. He was glad to find here so many of his own countrymen,

H

and a *strong* sympathy sprung **up** between them ; for no man can **love a** friend with a warmer heart than can a brother Irishman. He had a wide field to cultivate, with **a great** many appointments, and his labor was sometimes enough to tax to its utmost strength his fine, strong constitution.

He invariably took three appointments on Sabbath, and often five evenings of the week besides he was ready to hold forth the lamp of life to the people. He was blessed **with** some very gracious revivals of religion **while in Cavan ;** in which the leading members of the circuit took a prominent **part.** Some few of his people there were very emotional, especially during the time of revivals amongst them, and often their peculiar gestures and frantic shouts would almost terrify him.

He was altogether unaccustomed to this kind of thing, and felt it his duty to try and, if possible, effect a reform in this particular. But as these eccentricities were cherished as the peculiar operations of the Spirit of God, and held amongst the sacred things, to interfere with **which was** looked upon, by these friends, as a means of **retarding** the work of the Lord, he gave up in utter despair of convincing them **that the** Lord was not the author of confusion, but of **order.** He therefore allowed the matter to take its own course, bearing in mind that their sincerity might be harmonized with his, in the language of Paul, " Let every man be fully persuaded in his *own* mind." **He was,** upon the whole, very successful **there, and the people were** very kind to himself and family, and were ever regarded as amongst his truest and best friends. Towards the close of his last year he wrote to the *Evangelical Witness*, the organ of the conference, as follows :—

"Cavan, February 14, 1854.

"DEAR BROTHER,—I am happy to inform you that our missionary meetings on this circuit have been very good, and when the collectors have done their duty, the proceeds will be considerably in advance of last year.

"Our quarterly meeting was held 15th last month ; congregation about four hundred ; and we had a very good sermon by Rev. William Robinson, on The Nature and Efficacy of Prayer. The love feast was truly a time of refreshing, from the presence of the Lord ; the experience of many told that they were growing in grace, and in the knowledge of our Lord and Saviour Jesus Christ ; and about one hundred partook of the memorials of the dying love of our Redeemer.

"Our friends here are about building a small chapel in Cavanville, and also a parsonage-house, and are subscribing liberally towards both. So that, thank God, we are making some progress.

"W. GUNDY."

He remained two years in Cavan, and left it, with the many friends made there, for his next field of labor, which was the Oxford circuit, situated on the Rideau Canal. The conference which appointed him to this eastern part of the work was held at Hamilton, in June, 1854. This was a long move, but the greater part of the journey was accomplished by boat—from Port Hope to Kingston, and from thence to their circuit on the Rideau Canal. Here he` had also a large field to cultivate; and, apart from his circuit duties, he was compelled to meet and confront a host of ranting Millerites, who were diligent in berating the regular Gospel ministers, as well as agitating the people's minds, and on the ground of their peculiar doctrines were forming societies of their own; and, as most of these erratic sects do, they were connecting their converts with this new-fangled system by the—as we think—human invention of baptism by immersion. Mr. Gundy was then in the prime of his manhood, and being very clear, especially on the doctrines of Scripture, he was not long in putting these men to silence. Amongst his sermons I find some few which were evidently preached about this time, but the present design of this work prevents their introduction here. The state of the work on this circuit may be, to a certain extent, gathered from the following, recorded by himself, and is dated March 28th, 1856, only a few weeks before conference:—

"Our next meetings were on this circuit. Our love feast was a refreshing season indeed. Brother Doel preached a very excellent sermon, under which I sat with exquisite delight. Brother Baskerville preached in the evening at Jameson's school house, and Brother Doel at Oxford Mills, to large congregations. Our first missionary meeting was at Oxford Mills, where no missionary meeting has been held before, and where we have but six members, yet the subscriptions were very excellent. We have there a fine respectable congregation in general, and the offer of a lot of land from Richard Waugh, Esq., on which to build a chapel. Our next meeting was at Spencerville, and although we have but one member in that village, the subscriptions were more than last year. The storms prevented us from holding one meeting, and also caused the others to be thinly attended ; but I hope when the collectors perform their duty, the proceeds will exceed last year."

The following extracts from letters to one of his sons, will give us some idea of the subjects which frequently occupied his mind. These passages will let us into the heart of a father, yearning for the spiritual welfare of his children ; and also that of the intelligent Christian minister, interested in the prosperity of his church, his country and his fellow-men. The first is dated Oxford, 8th Dec., 1855 :—

" As you will be driven about from place to place," he says, "and will have a variety of characters to meet with, you must take the Saviour's advice to be as wise as a serpent and as harmless as a dove. You will need much of the grace of God, and consequently faithful prayer for those supplies of grace. You may rest assured that while you acknowledge the Lord in all your ways, He will direct your steps. I should hope that you will find many friends, but remember that Christ is a friend that sticketh closer than a brother. I suppose we will hear no more from the Cavan people, unless you may sometimes call and see

them. I have certainly a great regard for the Cavan
folks."

Thirteen days later in the same month, he says, "I hope
and pray (indeed we never forget you before a throne of
grace) that the great and mighty God, for the sake of His
Son, may open up your way. We have reason to thank
God for our health and all the blessings of this life.
Mother never enjoyed, for many years, better health."

On the first of March, of the same year, referring to the
necessity **for the** Cavan circuit receiving the services of a
good and efficient preacher, he says of the qualifications
of ministers :—"Our preachers ought to be men of reading, good grammarians, well read in church history, correct
theologians, good logicians, and so forth, in order to keep
pace with the times. You will think I am giving you a
lecture on preaching, but if I could speak as freely on
tanning (he to whom the letter was addressed was then a
tanner and currier), I would do so. Indeed **a** preacher
of the gospel ought to acquaint himself with all kinds of
knowledge."

In the same letter he continues :—" We should be very
thankful that we are not now at the Crimea; but even
here persons are suffering the loss of limbs. One man
near this lost his toes from the effects of frost. This is a
very severe climate, yet I have worn nothing but thin
calfskin boots and one pair of socks all this winter. But,
as you know, I take a splendid cold bath every morning."

CHAPTER X.

LAKE ERIE MISSION — LOUTH, TALBOTVILLE AND LONDON
NORTH CIRCUITS.

E may say, with considerable propriety, that **Mr.** Gundy had just reached the middle of life, although he **was** about **63** years old, when **he** bid adieu to the friends of the Oxford circuit. He had reached, at least, that period when the realities of the minister's life-work were pressing upon him with all the weight of their importance. The sentimentalism of youth, the love of poetry and eloquence, of fine philosophical distinctions and rhetorical paintings, were, in his mind, borne down by the pressure of the weight and value of souls, which was resting upon him.

His was an active life, and he was now in the midst of its toils. But this was his normal condition; and he could not rest at ease while men were every day perishing around him. His circuits were now fully realizing the value of his zeal, as men were, through its exercise, led to Christ. Bonar's beautiful lines express his oft repeated sentiments, and open up to us the great motives from which he acted :—

> " Go labor on ; spend, and be spent,—
> Thy joy to do the Father's will ;
> It is the way the Master went,
> Should not the servant tread it still ?

" Go labor on ; 'tis not for nought ;
  Thy earthly loss is heavenly gain ;
Men heed thee, love thee, praise thee not ;
  The Master praises,—what are men ?

" Go labor on, while it is day ;
  The world's dark night is hastening on ;
Speed, speed thy work, cast sloth away ;
  It is not thus that souls are won.

" Men die in darkness at your side,
  Without a hope to cheer the tomb ;
Take up the torch, and wave it wide,—
  The torch that lights time's thickest gloom.

" Toil on, faint not, keep watch, and pray ;
  Be wise, the erring soul to win ;
Go forth into the world's highway,
  Compel the wanderer to come in·

" Toil on, and in thy toil rejoice ;
  For toil comes rest, for exile home ;
Soon shalt thou hear the bridegroom's voice—
  The midnight peal—Behold, I come."

Mr. Gundy went up to the conference in June, 1856, which was held in Mallorytown, and from this he received another long move—from Oxford to Lake Erie mission.

On this mission he remained three years, and had the unspeakable pleasure of three years of prosperous toil. The records of his stay on this circuit are more numerous than any which have yet come to hand. The country near Haldimand was generally considered very unhealthy, and, indeed, so it proved to a portion of Mr. Gundy's family. The low, flat land, for several months of the year covered with water, and then left exposed to the scorching summer sun, resulted in filling the air with miasmatic vapors, and the people were suffering from ague, and the endless variety of fevers peculiar to such localities. Although, in common with those who had lived there for many years, nearly all the family were compelled to suffer from fever and ague, yet he was mercifully preserved, and was found at his post. The three years of his stay passed very pleasantly, and what adds more than ordinary pleasure to his lot, from the very first he was successful in winning souls. On December 1st, of his first year, he thus writes to the *Evangelical Witness*, describing a revival meeting with which they were graciously favoured :—

"LAKE ERIE MISSION,

"Haldimand, Dec. 1st, 1856.

"DEAR BROTHER,—It is with heartfelt gratitude to Almighty God that I send a few lines to the *Witness*, of a gracious outpouring of the Holy Spirit which we have witnessed for some weeks past, and are still enjoying.

"On the first Sabbath evening of last month, we commenced a protracted meeting here. With regard to myself, I must say, it was with fear and trembling, as we had no official member, except one leader, on the Mission ; but we remembered that it is not by might nor by power, but by my Spirit, saith the Lord.

"Night after night the congregations increased. The second week, I was providentially assisted by my son, Samuel B., from Yorkville, who intended to spend only a few days with us ; but such was the cry of sinners for mercy, and of backsliders to be restored to God's favor, that we constrained him to spend almost two weeks with us.

"I never, so far as I can judge, saw a more genuine work of God, and persons who are well informed were led to say truly, this is the work of God.

"There was no confusion. Penitents, indeed, were pleading with God, through the meritorious blood of the Lamb, for mercy; and justified persons praising God for the consolation. Otherwise, such was the deep solemnity of the audience, that if a pin had dropped it almost could be heard, and as only one prayed at a time, and as those who prayed seemed as if inspired from on high, the whole congregation was bowed into the deepest stillness, and the presence and power of God filled the house.

"Twenty-five persons were united yesterday morning to our little class, all professing to have received peace with God by faith in our Lord Jesus Christ, and some unspeakably happy in God,—to God be all the praise.

"My dear brother, the fields around us are ripe already to the harvest. Openings on every hand, our scriptural system preferred; but what is one minister in such a case. Several young men have been converted at our meeting; may God qualify some of them for the work of the ministry.—Amen."

In these genuine revivals of religion his soul delighted, and it was always noticeable in him, that he tried as much as possible to give prominence in the work, and the praise at its completion, to Jesus Christ, and Him crucified.

Sometime towards the close of his last year on this field, he sent the following lines to the *Witness*, which will, perhaps, give a full and satisfactory report from the circuit, and, together with the report of the first year and its glorious revival, will show how earnestly he was labouring and how well he was being rewarded for it :—

"I stated on a former occasion, that when I came here, I found this mission as low as it could be. There were only two or three members in the village of Haldimand, and certainly the other appointments were no better. But, thank God, in due time, our congregation steadily increased, and in my 1st and 2nd years, we were favored with some revivals ; and, although we have not the prosperity that we ardently desire at all our appointments, thanks to the Most High, we had a most blessed outpouring of the Holy Spirit at Haldimand village, at a protracted meeting last winter held there. Backsliders were reclaimed, and believers edified, and some remarkable conversions to God resulted therefrom. Two men, who were great drunkards, have been converted to God, and are now not only setting a godly example to their families, and laboring for their spiritual and temporal welfare, but are useful members of the church of God. We have in this class thirty well-established members, and seven on trial. To God be all the glory !

"I intend, as soon as the roads admit, to hold a protracted meeting at Port Maitland, where we have some excellent members, who are praying for and expecting a baptism from on high.

"We have also a lodge of Good Templars, so that drunkenness is fast disappearing from our village.

"Our friends gave us a donation last winter, which did well, considering the state the roads were in then. Indeed, we have had our share of mud this winter.

"Our missionary meetings were held according to appointment, and we had our quarterly meetings at the same time. The Sabbath services were truly refreshing. We had a most excellent and eloquent sermon from Brother Bettes; and both brethren had good congregations in the evening. The meetings through the week were well attended. Our people here are comparatively poor; we have no rich farmers or merchants, but a laboring class of people, and yet, I am glad to say, the subscription lists are more than double what they were last year."

The following conference—that of June, 1859—gave him an appointment to the Louth circuit, where he remained but one year; and, not finding it a congenial field of labor, he, at his own request, was removed to another.

The conference of 1860, which was held in Copetown, on the Ancaster circuit, gave him an appointment to the Talbotville circuit. This village, which contained the principal appointment on the circuit, was situated on the North Street, about three miles from the town of St. Thomas. He found the circuit in a very sad condition indeed. It had been rent through former troubles, which need not be called up here. They are past, and, I hope, buried in oblivion with all the train of associated evils. Mr. Gundy began his work here as in former places, by being determined to know nothing among men "save Jesus Christ, and Him crucified;" and he was soon appreciated as a man of God, whose chief aim it was to arrest the careless, strengthen the weak, and confirm the faithful, by the old, yet efficient, means of preaching the Gospel. While here he was instrumental in gaining for the church a good position, and in building up the people of God in the holy faith. During the three years of his stay he made many very warm and firm friends; and it was with great reluctance they parted with himself and family when the time of his appointment had expired.

In his correspondence during his stay here I find many subjects, of more or less interest, treated in his usual simple and candid manner, and all giving an idea of the nature of his trust in God, which, I may venture to say, was indicated in connection with the small as well as the more important matters of life. In a letter to his son James, dated Talbotville, February 14th, 1861, he thus gives an account of an unpleasant journey which he and Mrs. Gundy made from Hamilton to the above-mentioned place, a distance of about one hundred miles:—

"I am happy to tell you that we got through to brother Eddy's, on the Waterford circuit, from Hamilton, about thirty-five miles; but it was dreadful travelling, the storm all the way in our faces. My eyes were sealed up with ice almost all the way, so that I could scarcely see the *horse.* We got right into a drift at night, about half a mile from our destination, but, thank God, we were not frozen at all. Mother had a cold before she left Samuel's, and took a severe influenza by facing the storm, but she is now better. We had to remain at Mr. Eddy's on Friday, and on Saturday drove to Aylmer, to Mr. Bell's circuit, and got home about eleven o'clock on Sunday morning, horse and all worn down. We travelled on Saturday fifty miles, on Sunday fifteen, and I was able to fill my appointment at noon. We are now comfortable, thanks to the Most High."

On April 13th, 1863, he thus writes to James, sympathising and advising with him:—

"Yours of **the 6th** inst. gave us much pleasure on the one hand and sorrow on the other—sorrow, that you have overworked yourself to the injury of your constitution; and pleasure, that the work of the Lord is reviving on your circuit so extensively. We should regard Mr. Wesley as a good judge of human nature; and one of his most particular injunctions to his preachers was to avoid loud speaking and loud singing, and to close every meeting in one hour, if they had any regard for their health, and had any desire to live any length of time to serve their Maker and save souls; and it is an undoubted fact that many young men, by not taking such advice and acting upon it, have lessened their days and cut short their usefulness. You ought certainly to have given up your meeting sooner than be obliged to retire from the work of God prematurely. If you take care of your health, you may yet **live** many years to preach the everlasting Gospel; and I do most solemnly, in the fear of God, request that you will try to speak, pray, and sing more calmly. Spare yourself, that you may live to glorify God, and be of use for many years yet to come."

It was during the second year of his stay on this circuit that the writer became personally acquainted with him. He was then in the flower of a green old age, and could endure almost any amount of physical labour, and his intellect was as clear and strong as ever. His letter to the *Witness* is as follows :—

"TALBOTVILLE CIRCUIT.

"MR. EDITOR : DEAR SIR,—I am sure it will give pleasure to yourself and many of the readers of the *Witness* to know that this circuit is still advancing in the right direction. This was very fully manifested on last Sabbath and the Monday following. On the Sabbath, a field meeting was held in the Gore, when a very large and attentive congregation was convened to hear words whereby they might be saved. Sermons were delivered in the forenoon by Rev. M. Silcocks (Congregational), and the writer, and in the afternoon by Rev. S. B. Gundy and Yokom (Episcopal). It was a most beautiful day, the congregations highly respectable, and a most excellent choir. Oh, how delightful thus to spend the sacred day of the Lord, to sound his praises, and proclaim his gospel in nature's temple, under the canopy of Heaven, and surrounded by the stately trees of the forest.

"On Monday, a tea meeting was held in the same place, when a good number sat down at two o'clock, p.m., to a splendid repast, gratuitously provided by the friends of the neighbourhood. Full justice was done by about two hundred persons to the sumptuous provisions, and seven baskets full remained. Excellent addresses were delivered by Revs. S. B. Gundy, Yokom (Episcopal), Wm. Webb, and J. Caswell. Mr. Caswell's address was listened to with the deepest attention, especially that part which referred to his visit to the old country.

"Proceeds between thirty and forty dollars.

"Sept. 30, 1862." " WILLIAM GUNDY.

The people were very much attached to him as a preacher, but, if anything, more so as a man. The three years of his allotted time, however, sped swiftly away, as does time always when we are amongst congenial companions ; and while the people sorrowed on account of his departure, the preacher was none the less sad, and both felt that the sacred Poet's language finely expressed their feelings :—

" Blest be the dear uniting love,
   Which will not let us part ;
Our bodies may far off remove,
   We still are one in heart.

Joined in one spirit to our head,
   Where He appoints we go ;
And still in Jesus' footsteps tread,
   And do His work below.

O may we ever walk in Him,
   And nothing know beside,
Nothing desire, nothing esteem,
   But Jesus crucified."

The next conference was held in Owen Sound, in June, 1863, from which he was appointed to the London north circuit. This was a large field, and embraced a part of two or three townships north of London. It was **too** large altogether for one man to work to advantage, but to make up for this he was supplied with a colleague each of the three years he was there, with whom he worked in harmony, and their joint labours resulted in much good to the circuit. Although no man for unhealthy excitement, **yet** he was ready to do his utmost in *special* efforts **for** the conversion of sinners. In these meetings he laboured very hard, frequently having to drive several miles after night ; and, as is a well known fact, in that part of the country the roads are the muddiest of the muddy **in** the spring **and** fall **of** the year ; but nothing but a physical impossibility could prevent him from being present at his appointments.

While on this circuit he was instrumental in the building of a church in the township of Nissouri, and the field, which was in a very disorganized state when he found it, **began** to assume the order and working shape which he always laboured to produce. The classes, which had been allowed to go without any proper arrangement or order of meeting, and the various courts of the church peculiar to our polity, were all fixed in a working and business-like shape.

In the month of March of his last year in London North, he wrote to the *Witness* as follows :—

" As you are receiving information of a pleasing nature

I

from many circuits, I would like to say a few words in reference to this circuit, and first, I am glad to say that the
friends at Hunt's appointment are now prepared, as soon
as the spring appears, to build a brick church. They
have obtained a deed of a lot of land in a very suitable
place, the stones, brick, lumber, timber, sand, &c., &c.,
are all on the ground and paid for. It will be 26 x 36
feet, with gothic windows; will be finished off in the
best style, and, best of all, without a cent of debt. Although **the** brethren in that locality are not the most
wealthy, and but a few families, yet the principle they go
upon is this, that ministers ought not to be taxed to pay
for the building of churches for the people any longer;
and I am sure, Mr. Editor, you will say they are perfectly
right on this point.

"The subscriptions to our missionary funds, after the
collectors have done their part, will, we hope, be in
advance of last year. The friends at Birr got up a tea
meeting, which was well attended; provisions were of the
best and richest kind, such as the ladies of the London
north circuit can get up. The Bryanston choir charmed
the audience, and the proceeds were over forty dollars.
While I was attending **the missionary** meetings, brother
Robinson was engaged in holding protracted meetings.
He laboured hard. I hope and pray that fruit may yet
appear. **Our** last quarterly meeting was the best every
way we had this year. Thus, Sir, we are trying to get on,
and the best of all is, God is with us.

"Yours truly,
"WILLIAM GUNDY."

Later in the same year—the last—he made another report through the connexional organ. This article, which we give below, is probably the last he ever wrote for the *Witness;* and it will show, to some extent, the nature of the prosperity he enjoyed there, and the subjects referred to evidently indicate the channel in which his mind and interests in the work of God ran :—

"LONDON NORTH CIRCUIT.

"MR. EDITOR,—I am sure it will be very gratifying to the readers of the *Witness*, who are acquainted with the London north circuit, to know that it is in a very much improved state. It is true that conversions to God are not so numerous as we could desire; but there have been, thank God, some, and several persons have, under the preaching of the Gospel, been awakened to a sense of their sinful state.

"At a protracted effort at Zion Church, Fitzgerald's, the church was every night crowded to excess. Some four or five persons united with us there, and the members were generally blessed. A tea meeting was held soon afterwards, the proceeds of which, after defraying expenses, amounted to $31. Our next protracted effort was at Hunt's School House, and, if possible, was still more interesting. The place was crowded every night ; the deepest solemnity pervaded the congregation, and the greatest attention was paid to the preaching of the word. Several persons, heads of families, and young people, united with us, and we expect others to do so. The friends have also determined to erect a church, which will give greater permanency to our cause in the neighbourhood. I am glad to say that brother Keam, my respected colleague, laboured faithfully and efficiently in these meetings; indeed, he is a good and faithful brother, and beloved by all the circuit.

"On Wednesday, February 22nd, a tea meeting was held in the brick church, which was very successful. Good eatables provided by the ladies; good music by the Bryanston choir; and good speeches, made the evening pass very pleasantly.

"The proceeds, amounting to over $32, were applied for the benefit of the ministers on the circuit. On Wednesday evening, March 8th, a tea meeting was held at Bryanston, which was also very successful, the amount realized, after paying expenses, being considerably over $30. We are at present engaged in holding another **protracted** meeting at Cunningham's. Already have we felt the presence of the Master with us, and we expect that much **good** will result from the meeting, both in the conversion **of** sinners and the edification of the church.

"**There** is good material on this circuit to work upon, and nothing **to** prevent it from becoming **one** of the best circuits in our connexion; and, if a man of prudence and energy be appointed as my successor next year, I am persuaded that he shall not have to labour in vain, or spend his strength for naught.

"WM. GUNDY."

In a letter to his son, Samuel, then stationed in Mon

treal, dated London North, 22nd March, 1866, he thus
writes :—

"We are looking out for a visit from the Fenians. If
they come, they surely will not get back so easily. How
do you feel about them in Montreal ? I hope and pray
that God may put a hook in their jaw and a bridle in
their mouth, and say, thus far shall you go, and no further.
However, for my part, I have no fear. God has always
confounded them, and He sits at the helm ; and if He be
for us, who can injure us ? There is one thing to fear,
however : Popery has been fostered too much in England.
God, no doubt, raised England high in the scale of nations that she might perfect the Reformation, and uphold
the circulation of His word ; but she has taken the serpent into her bosom, and she may expect to be stung. I
pray that it may not be to the death."

In the same letter, he speaks of their trials, occasioned
especially by their son, William's, sickness with some
dreadful fever. In speaking of the future, he says, in the
same letter, "Well, we will be soon looking out for conference, and it will be trying till we know our destination.
I hope we will get some small circuit ; but we must leave
all in the hands of God. All will be right when He di-
rects the way." It was the habit of his life to cultivate a
cheerful, hopeful, thankful spirit, and, though often cast
down, he was never discouraged. It was always a great
pleasure to him to anticipate the happy family gatherings
with which we were favoured at conference times ; and he
seemed instinctively led, at these times, to review the

mercies of God during the past. In view of approaching conference time, he thus wrote to us from London North : " Dear children, I must have done. If we can be nearer next year, so as to see one another sometimes, it will be very gratifying indeed. Conference will soon be on, and I trust we shall all have a very happy meeting. I hope and pray that we may continue to enjoy good health, and especially the favor and peace of God, which is the best of all. This circuit is much improved. We had some very good protracted meetings, and some additions to the membership, and we have abundance of provisions ; so that, with good health and sound mind, and Christ in us the hope of glory, we have every reason to thank God, take courage, and run the race set before us with alacrity and delight."

CHAPTER XI.

DOMESTIC COMFORTS — WATERFORD CONFERENCE — MIDDLETON AND LINDSAY CIRCUITS.

ARE says:—"To Adam, Paradise was a *home*. To the *good* of his descendants, *home* is a *paradise*."

Such was Mr. Gundy's home. There he was the soul of his family's happiness.

The six years spent in the neighbourhood of London form a bright spot in his earthly journey. In some respects the brightest. In his early days the gush of religious fervour, added to the bright exuberant joy of youth, made the time one long to be remembered. But since then the maturity of manhood had been reached, and he was now descending the hill of time ; and at evening time he was to enjoy a glorious light. He always much enjoyed the society of his children, and was now so situated that the pleasure of their company might be frequently realized. They were no longer the merry little ones that years ago had

"Filled his house with glee ;"

For the same hand which had multiplied his years, had hurried *them* on towards middle life. While living at Talbotville and London North, Mr. and Mrs. Gundy again and again were cheered by these welcome visits. Samuel was stationed on the St. Mary's circuit, James in Strathroy, Joseph in London city, John at Komoko, we in Ingersoll, and William—the only son not in the ministry—was living in London, and Ellen (Mrs. Pearson), the farthest away, in Brampton. These constituting the whole family were permitted to share the joy of those days. The walls of the paternal dwelling often resounded with the hearty laugh of children at home, and ever and anon with the song of praise and voice of prayer. Those were days when it were hard to say who—parents or children—most enjoyed the consecrated hour of domestic bliss. No one could more appreciate such occasions than himself, and it seemed as if, to him, the very climax of human happiness were then reached. The head of gray hairs was a crown of glory in that family.

After leaving London North, we were more widely scattered, and such opportunities as above referred to were attended with greater expense and inconvenience. Such are some of the disadvantages of the itinerancy.

The conference which was held in 1866, was in many respects one long to be remembered. It began its sittings on Wednesday morning, 6th of June, in the quiet little village of Waterford, surrounded as it is by a beautifully improved country, which is dotted with the stately mansions of princely farmers. The magnificent scenery of the place, and hearty welcome of the people, compensated in a good degree for the long journey from the railway; but it is not in these respects alone that this is marked as a conference long to be remembered. The country was in a great heat of excitement on account of the Fenian invasion of our soil, and the reports which were continually circulating through the land were calculated to thrill the heart of every lover of his country with anxiety for her safety. Those vile miscreants, from no other motives for their work than to avenge supposed wrongs which they had suffered at the hands of Great Britain, were threatening our lives. The regular army and the volunteers were rushing to and fro as necessity or report might call them ; but, thanks to a merciful Providence, these marauders and murderers were neither successful in taking the land themselves, nor in originating a state of disturbance between Canada and the United States, either of which, I presume, they would **have re**joiced to have effected.

In the midst of this excitement the representatives of the connexion, to the number of **one** hundred and fourteen, were found sufficiently interested in the churches' welfare to leave their homes, and make the necessary sacrifices to meet each other, in order to realize the objects **of** our annual conference. Another circumstance which contributed to make that a memorable conference, was the fact that we were here favoured with the first official appearance of the Rev. William Cocker amongst us, who, on coming, was honoured by an American University with the title of Doctor of Divinity. The Dr. was elected without a dissenting voice to the office of president of conference, and those who were present to hear his inaugural address will never forget it as long as they live.

The honest open countenance, sound advice and eloquent sermons of a live Englishman added much to the general interest of the gathering.

Another remarkable and ever to-be-remembered circumstance was the delightful love-feast enjoyed on the morning of Sabbath, June 10th, 1866. The writer was somewhat late in arriving at this meeting, but such was the holy influence which filled the house that, although only enabled barely to get inside the door, he was, as by the power of an unseen but felt influence, melted into tears of gladness and joy. I think I never realized anything like it either before or since. The Lord was there manifested to our hearts as he does not manifest himself to the world. In the report of Dr. Cocker to the English missionary committee, he thus refers to the meeting, and to the subject of this work, who was honoured as one of its leaders:—

" The services held during the conference were very numerously attended, and were characterized by a high degree of holy excitement. Again and again we were constrained to exclaim, ' Master, it is good for us to be here.' Emphatically may this be said of the love-feast which was held at eight o'clock on the Sabbath morning. It was the first time I had attended a love-feast at so early an hour, and I confess I went with a feeling of strangeness. When I reached the chapel, an aged minister, who has three sons and a son-in-law in our ministry, was opening the service. His very venerable appearance, his radiant countenance, and the simplicity and fervour of his remarks, at once arrested my attention, and before father Gundy had done speaking, I forgot the unusual hour of the love-feast, and felt that we had come to the gate of Heaven. I cannot, by any words, give you an adequate idea of the grace and glory that crowned this consecrated hour of Christian fellowship. The speaking was remarkable for its reference to departed friends. The hearts of some had been stricken by the loss of their children, and they still mourned ; but lovely visions shone through their tears. They spoke of their little ones as flowers blooming in Paradise, and rejoiced in the hope of a time when they will see them in fairer forms than even parental love ever imagined. As many touching allusions of this kind were made, all seemed to realize the full force and sweetness of the words we often sing :—

> " E'en now by faith we join our hands
> With those who went before,
> And greet the blood-besprinkled bands
> On the eternal shore."

"Since our conference love-feast at Liverpool, I have not attended one so rich in spiritual influence as this. The friends were not willing to separate without an arrangement to have it resumed, and it was continued after the preaching and sacramental services in the evening with the same hallowed feelings, and thus a happy day was happily concluded."

Another circumstance which distinguished the Waterford conference was the fact that we were short of young men for filling up the appointments, and it was found necessary to station two married preachers on some of the circuits. In the case of **Mr.** Gundy, the stationing committee thought it would relieve him of some considerable care and responsibility to place him on one of those circuits, for it was evident to himself and others that he was approaching the evening of life's day. He was therefore sent to the Middleton circuit. This appointment, although made with the best and purest intentions towards him, did not result altogether according to the expectations of his best friends, for it turned out that the field was a very large one; and although the mental labour was necessarily less, the physical was much more. His very intimate and much beloved friend, the Rev. James Caswell, was the superintendent of the circuit, and upon him chiefly rested the charge of managing its affairs, while Mr. Gundy held the honorary position of chairman of the district. The former resided in Simcoe, and the **latter in Delhi.**

Mr. Caswell, who had known him long and familiarly, showed him every possible consideration of kindness in his power, and, although the year was one of no ordinary degree of trial to both, they were happy in each other's society, and in their joint service in the Master's vineyard.

This circuit was in a very backward state, and neither of them received the full allowance of salary. The difficulties of the circuit were much increased on account of sickness on Mrs. Gundy's part, and gross neglect on that of the people, for whom, both himself and Mr. Caswell worked with the utmost zeal and faithfulness. In a letter dated 24th of January, 1867, in which he speaks of their trials and privations, " I do hope," he says, " we shall be able to live out a few months more. Mother has suffered very much from bilious attacks this fall. It certainly is a very sickly part of the country. Some of the friends at Simcoe made a social, and the proceeds were about $14. It was just before Christmas. I was to preach there the Sabbath before Christmas, and I assure you it gladdened my heart to receive five dollars. I went immediately and bought some of the best beef I could obtain, hoping we might have a good Christmas dinner; but when I came home I found mother in bed shaking with ague, and Fred,"—his grandson, about five years old—" minding her."

In November, 1866, he wrote, not in the spirit of complaint; but, in the letter, bare, stubborn facts are related, which will give a pretty correct idea of the trials through which they passed during most of that year. He says,—"I delayed writing till after our quarterly meeting, in order to remit you a dollar. I received seven dollars in silver, and, although I tried to get a bill in this village, it was in vain. As soon as I get a dollar bill I will send it. We are both much better, thank God. Our meeting was held in Simcoe, a poor business meeting indeed. I never saw Mr. Caswell so discouraged. They never had such preachers, they say, and that ought to suffice; as to a support, that is another question! Our missionary meetings are next week. I don't expect much." The brief period of their stay on this circuit was certainly the darkest in his ministerial career. They hailed the coming of conference with great delight, and, bidding adieu to the friends and the trials there, they left to mingle in the joy of friendly greeting which awaited them in the home of their son-in-law, Mr. Henry Pearson, near Brampton, where several of their children had gathered to meet them.

As we were stationed in Ingersoll, thirty miles from Delhi, it gave us great pleasure to be able to go and see them occasionally, and have them visit us, a privilege which no one could better appreciate than my dear departed father-in-law. He was, at the conference of 1867, stationed on the Lindsay circuit, a field little better suited to his failing condition. By undertaking the work of packing and shipping their goods for them, they were enabled to move pretty comfortably ; and, during the first year on the circuit, Mr. Gundy seemed to retain his vigor very well. He preached in the town of Lindsay, where, nearly twenty years before, he held forth the word of life, while he was connected with the Brock circuit. At the suggestion of the stationing committee he resided in the country, nearly ten miles from the town. As he was surrounded by numbers of his people where he lived, it was impossible for him to devote the necessary attention to Lindsay, and after a while the appointment was dropped. During the fall of his first year, he met with a very serious accident, which no doubt impaired his usefulness, and hastened his end. He had driven over to the house of one of his members, a distance of about three-fourths of a mile from the place of his residence, and when he was coming home, on leaving the yard, he was compelled to pass over a bar, about nine inches high, which had been left in the gateway. His pony being very spirited and restive, dashed over this break-neck affair at full speed, and threw him out on his head and shoulders, when she ran home alone with the buggy. Shortly afterwards, Mrs. Gundy, finding the pony at the gate, turned her around and went back in search of Mr. Gundy. She found him coming leisurely along the road; and, when interrogated as to how he got the fall, or the extent of his injury, he seemed to have no knowledge of the event. All recollection of the particulars of the **circum**stance seemed to have left him, and, save a few bruises on the side of his face, arm and side, he appeared none the worse. However, about two weeks after he was attacked with partial paralysis of the same side, from which he gradually recovered. But before the conference, he was again attacked with the same trouble. We all wanted him to retire from the work and try, if possible, and spend the remainder of his days amongst us, in quiet retirement from the great activities which had employed him all the years of his life. But he could not bear the idea of giving up an employment in which he so much delighted.

Many years before, he had expressed the wish " to die n the harness," and he seemed still inspired with the same desire. He was present at the next conference held in London, in 1868, and was again appointed to the same field; but it was now evident that he was failing very fast.

Although he was at one time about fourteen months without a return of paralysis, yet we could see evident indications of a change in his appearance. He was growing quite helpless in body, and his brain was less active than formerly. In writing us during the time of this loss of strength, he complained of his head. He said,—" I would have written before this, but I find my head going round, and I must forego the pleasure I once enjoyed in writing." It was a happy circumstance for both himself and Mrs. Gundy that they were living within a short distance of their son Joseph, whose attention, together with that of his amiable wife, was unremitting.

They did all in their power to help in the working of his circuit, and also in the management of his domestic concerns, and thereby lightened his heart, while they lessened his labour. It was a circumstance for which neither the father nor the son could be too thankful. If they had been far from any of their children, they certainly could never have received the attention from strangers which their son and his wife were only too glad to be able to render.

At the expiration of their time—two years—they had fully resolved to come, at our repeated solicitations, and live the remainder of their days with us, an honour which we were proud to enjoy. It will be remembered by those who saw him at the Waterdown conference, in 1869, how very much he had failed, and how in body and mind he seemed to be sinking. It was with great difficulty he managed to make the journey from **near Omemee** to that conference. He would certainly have felt it **a** greater affliction to have been kept away, than all the suffering he endured to get there. He delighted in meeting his fellow travellers and fellow labourers in the annual convocations of the church. We were then on the Milton circuit, and resided quite near our church, in that quiet little town ; and after a little visiting around amongst their sons, they came to Milton to settle down **and** rest in peace the remainder of their days, which with him was not very long. Upon **their first** coming, I felt it to be my duty to ask him into the pulpit, **and get him** to close the meeting with prayer, **but the** repeated attacks of the trouble, induced **by the** fall above referred **to,** soon prevented **him from** taking any leading part **in the** services of **the sanctuary, and** this he **felt to** be a great affliction indeed, for **upwards of fifty years he had** thus been employed, and his soul delighted in **the work.**

But still he continued to attend the service, and the **class** meeting he esteemed a great delight. Any position in the church was, to him, honourable, and much to **be** desired. The language **of the** Psalmist **fully expressed** his feelings towards **the** sanctuary, **and** often **became the** channel of his holiest emotions and most **devout gratitude.**

" How amiable are Thy tabernacles, O Lord of hosts ! my soul longeth, yea, even **fainteth** for the courts of the **Lord : my heart and my flesh crieth** out **for** the living

J

God.   For a day in Thy courts is better than a thousand.
I had rather be a door-keeper in the house of my God,
than to dwell in the tents of wickedness."   From this,
at times, his ideas became more or less confused, and it
was only at intervals that he could converse at any length
on the most familiar subjects.   His difficulty seemed to
be more in the tongue, which appeared partially para-
lyzed, than in his brain, and, what was very singular, he
could appreciate reading when performed by another, but
when done by himself he seemed to have no enjoyment
in it.   This was particularly the case with him the last
few months of his stay upon earth.

CHAPTER XII.

RESOLUTION OF THE WATERDOWN CONFERENCE—HIS
STAY AT MILTON—LAST SICKNESS AND DEATH.

HE aged servant, **weary** with the fatigue induced by years of **honest toil, is now to cease** his labour: **the veteran soldier** of the Cross, after many a hard-fought battle, is now to **lay** his armour down and rest a little **at** the door-step **of** his final home—just a little sojourn here, and then possess **his** blest inheritance forever—an inheritance bought with the **Saviour's blood.**

It was impossible that Mr. **Gundy should continue** longer in the active work. **He left it with reluctance, for** it was his greatest delight **to preach Christ to the people.** There was, **however, no alternative, and with undiminished** love **for the work** and for **the Saviour,** Jesus! he breathed **the words of acquiescence,** "Father, thy will **be done."**

The last conference Mr. Gundy ever attended was held at Waterdown, **in** June, 1869. During the sittings of this conference, the **following** resolution was passed, and was recorded in its **minutes :—**

"That while this conference accedes **to the request of** our venerable father, **the Rev.** William Gundy, in retiring from the active work of the ministry, it earnestly prays that his declining years may **be** crowned with the Divine favour; and that, when called **from this scene** of trial, he may hear the welcome voice of approval, 'Well done, good and faithful servant, enter thou into the joy of thy Lord !'"

We have referred to the beginning of his ministerial career, in the land of his birth; and his entering upon the full work of a Gospel minister in this country; the above resolution, passed by the unanimous vote of the conference, composed of nearly two hundred members, points to its close. Since he entered the ministry, with us, at the Cavan conference, held in the old ninth line chapel in 1849, what strange mutations have transpired in this world of bustle and care. Old father Time has passed along and left his mark on every person and thing around us. In that period of twenty-one years, the geography of this earth has been visibly changed. Nations, institutions, churches and men, have all felt the influence of his *magic wand.*

When Mr. Gundy began his duties as a Methodist New Connexion minister, the conference stationed forty-three men as active labourers ; and of that number I find, by comparing the *minutes* of 1849 with those of 1870, only seven remain in the same capacity now. These are the Rev. James Caswell, W. Preston, F. G. Weaver, D. D. Rolston, E. Williams, T. M. Jeffries, and W. Peck. The voices of the remaining thirty-six have been hushed, some of them in the silence of the grave, and others in the retirement of a superannuated relation. Only six of the thirty-six are found on the list of superannuated preachers, so that there are thirty gone, we know not where. Some of them, it is true, have crossed the flood, several are in other churches, while a few may have found their way back into secular employments. How solemn the admonition to us all! "Whatsoever thy hand findeth to do, do it with thy might; for there is no work, nor device, nor knowledge, nor wisdom, in the grave whither thou goest."

His was a long course of trial and service since first he joined the ranks of the local preachers at Tullamore, yet few there are who are enabled to carry through so many years an untarnished character and unsullied reputation. He was thankful to be able to sit down at evening, and look over life's short but eventful day; and then, with undiminished hope, to contemplate, in a little, "sitting down with Abraham, Isaac and Jacob, in the kingdom of heaven."

He had only a few months of his last year to spend with us. During the first part of his time at Milton, he could enjoy a drive or a walk into the country; but, after a little, he could no longer succeed in getting into the buggy, and his limbs refused to carry him very far on his afternoon walks. In the spring of 1870 he seemed to sink very fast. It was touching to see the old man of seventy-five years, with head as white as "the driven snow," sitting in his arm-chair, waiting and watching in silence for the coming of a friend in whom he confided. Mrs. Gundy, his ever-faithful and attentive partner, and who had been all along through life the willing sharer of his joys and sorrows, watched by his side continually.

In the days of his health, he was much given to close reading. Sometimes the philosopher or the poet engaged his attention; but now, the Bible alone, without note or comment, contained his choice fund of reading matter; —and, of the Scriptures, the New Testament seemed most precious, because it contained the most and best of Jesus. Mrs. Gundy read to him from day to day, for hours at a time, from a beautiful copy of the New Testament, in two volumes with large print, the gift of their sons James and Joseph. O, what comfort they gathered from those pages, no human tongue can tell; but the words of repeated assent and approval, which he gave to the truths of the Book of God, told how much he appreciated them. All that medical skill could do was but little; the time for the breaking up and dissolving of nature had come, and the pins of the earthly tabernacle were gradually giving way. The kindness of Dr. Street, the attending physician, will not soon be forgotten; he was ready at every call and gave his services freely as done unto the Lord. Sometimes Mr. Gundy was the subject of strong temptations from the evil one; and at one time in particular—a few weeks before his death—he had been greatly oppressed in mind most of the day, and was seized with an involuntary weeping for hours together. He could give no reason for it, otherwise than the feelings of mental depression under which he was labouring. Advised by his constant partner, they both retired into their closet to pray, and their special prayer was for help in this hour of weakness and trial; and, as they wrestled

on, the victory was gained. The wrestling Jacob became
again the prevailing Israel. The oppressed servant heard
his Master's voice, "My grace is sufficient for thee";
and oh, what comfort this answer brought ! Unspeakable
joy filled their souls; and he was, from that hour, left in
undisturbed possession of " the peace of God which
passeth all understanding." During the month of May
of the same year he was taken very ill. He seemed to
lose the use of his limbs, and was quite as helpless as a
child ; but, amidst it all, he retained his reason. As we
all expected, he could not survive many days, his children
were summoned to his bedside; but, as the time for
conference wore on, he became considerably better, and
we ventured away to the duties of our annual gathering.
I shall never forget the scene when his son James and
myself were starting away ; as we approached his bedside
to say farewell, **he gave us** such a look ! it seemed to say
I would like **to** go with **you** ; and his eyes filled with **tears
upon** the thought of being kept away from **an** annual
assemblage where **he** had been regularly **for** twenty years.
For a few weeks he gradually improved in strength, until
about **the** 18th of June, when he began again to sink.
As Mrs. Gundy, whose ever-watchful care could detect
the slightest change, noticed **this** sudden failure of
strength, she, **as was** her wont, **resorted to the Scriptures.**
She read a portion **of the** 15th chapter **of 1st** Corinthians,
and, **as** she came to that incomparably sublime passage,
" O Death, where is thy sting ? O Grave, where is thy
victory ? Thanks be to God who giveth us the victory

through our Lord Jesus Christ," she said, "Are not these blessed words?" He turned towards her, and, being unable to say more, he said, "Oh yes," while a heavenly smile lighted up his countenance, and his features appeared radiant from the overwhelming glories that filled his soul. In a short time he fell into a heavy sleep, from which he never awoke on earth. The most of his children were with him at this time; and, as the hours wore away, it became evident that he was gradually growing weaker, when about 11 o'clock on Tuesday night, June 21st, 1870, his spirit was released and entered into rest. I never before witnessed such a death-bed scene. We were deprived of the satisfaction of conversing with him to the last, or of having from his lips a dying testimony or farewell word; but we have the testimony of a life spent in the service of Christ, and an end as peaceful and calm as could be desired.

> "He laid his head on Jesus' breast,
> And breathed his life out sweetly there."

Immediately, as the spark of life had flown, the face assumed a most angelic appearance—a halo of soft heavenly light seemed to encircle that honored head, and the whole room was filled with the glory of the Lord. His lone partner, weak and weary with constant watching, was wonderfully sustained by the spirit of God; and, as if strength for the ordeal were given, and inspired with a rapturous view of the future, and a soul overflowing with the love of Christ, she gave expression to the following

words of spiritual submission and triumph : "Glory be to
the Father and to the Son and to the Holy Ghost."

> "The chamber where the good man meets his fate,
> Is privileged beyond the common walks of life.
> Quite on the verge of heaven."

The Rev. James McAlister—president of the conference
—attended the funeral, and preached the sermon which is
published with this memoir.   A goodly number of sym-
pathizing friends gathered at this service in the Methodist
New Connexion church in Milton.   The choir of the
church rendered, with good effect, the beautiful hymn, of
which the following are the words, so appropriate ; and,
as the servant of God dwelt upon the dying Christian and
his triumph over death, our hearts were **constrained to**
say,—" Let me die the death of the righteous, and let my
last end be like his :"

> " Go to **the** grave in all thy glorious prime,
>   In full activity of zeal and power ;
> A Christian cannot die before his **time,**
>   The Lord's appointment is the **servant's hour.**
>
> **"Go to the** grave; at eve from labor cease ;
>   Rest on thy sheaves, thy harvest work is done,
> Come from the heat of battle, and in peace,
>   Soldier go home ; with thee the fight is won.
>
> " Go to **the** grave, **for there** thy Saviour lay,
>   In death's embraces, ere he rose on high ;
> And all the ransom'd, by that narrow way,
>   Pass **to eternal** life beyond the sky.
>
> " Go **to** the grave ; no, take thy seat **above ;**
>   Be thy pure spirit present with the Lord,
> Where thou for faith and hope hast perfect love,
>   **And open** vision for the written word."

His remains were conveyed, in hearse, to Churchville, a distance of twelve miles. The body was carried carefully and slow to its last resting place by the following honoured brethren, of the Methodist N. C. Church :—Robert Hawthorne, George Brownridge, Logan McCann, Francis Reed, William Center and Donald McClaren.

In that beautiful cemetery, near the residence of his daughter—Mrs. Pearson—several of his grand-children lie sleeping. Around his grave a loving weeping company stood, and as the sexton finished his work, with **hearts filled with** sorrow and yet with hope, we joined in singing the beautiful hymn :—

> " I'm but a stranger here,
>   Heaven is my home ;
> Earth is a desert drear,
>   Heaven is my home ;
> Danger and sorrow stand,
> Round me on every hand ;
>   Heaven is my fatherland,
>   Heaven is my home ;
>
> " What though the tempest rage,
>   Heaven is my home ;
> Short is my pilgrimage,
>   Heaven is my home.
> Time's cold and wintry blast,
>   Soon will be overpast ;
> I shall reach home at last,
>   **Heaven is my home.**
>
> " Then at **my Saviour's side,**
>   Heaven **is** my home ;
> I shall be glorified,
>   Heaven is my home.
> There are the good and blest,
> Those I love most and best ;
> There, too, I soon shall rest,
>   Heaven is my home."

As the strains of that sacred song died away on the still air of that June evening, we turned away from the spot, and left the sleeping clay in hope of a happy meeting on the morning of the resurrection.

Thus we have tried to trace the life of one who had lived to see his 75th year; and there are few who were more evidently preserved and led by the guiding hand of the heavenly father.

CHAPTER XIII.

REV. JAMES WHITE'S LETTER—MR. GUNDY AN ORANGE-
MAN—IRELAND AND POPERY.

THE Rev. James White, of the Methodist New
Connexion conference, whose acquaintance with
Mr. Gundy was of considerable intimacy, and
that for a number of years, at our request to furnish any
facts he might have which would be of service in this
work, thus writes :—

" My acquaintance with the late Rev. W. Gundy commenced about the year 1831, in the town of Portarlington, Ireland. He was then engaged in the mercantile
business, with fair prospects of success ; his capital was
small, but his character for honesty and trustworthiness
stood high. He was a local preacher in good standing,
and was generally acceptable in his public ministrations.
It required a good deal of circumspection for a man to
deal with the public through the week, and then on the
Sabbath to preach to many of the same people, without
being charged with inconsistency, or perhaps hypocrisy.
But Mr. Gundy generally got credit for sincerity, and, as
a proof that he was liked, had good congregations. He generally preached twice on the Sabbath, and occasionally
through the week. In 1836 he moved to Mt. Mellick.
Here he was no stranger, as he used generally to preach
there every second Sabbath, the travelling preachers only

coming once a fortnight. Mt. Mellick, Portarlington, Maryboro, Monastereven, Rosenallis, &c., shared in his voluntary and accepted services. He deservedly had the confidence of the travelling ministers, and he and his noble wife gave them a cordial and hearty welcome to their house and board. He was no time server; he was a generous, warm-hearted Methodist.

"Methodism was unpopular, especially with the High Church party, who were rigid Calvinists. These branded Methodism as not merely the half-way house to Popery, but Popery itself, in its worst type. Many men would have abandoned a system that stood in the way of their temporal prosperity; but our late friend was made of sterner stuff. He loved Methodism, because through her instrumentality he was brought to God; he loved her doctrines because they clearly set forth the compassion of God, to every son and daughter of Adam, through Christ Jesus; he loved her simple form of worship, and especially rejoiced that the door of usefulness was thrown wide open to every man who gave proof of a sound conversion to God, from the simple prayer leader to the president of the conference. He had frequent controversies with the Calvinists of Portarlington, especially the ladies, who manifested great zeal to convert him from his false doctrine. It was amusing to see them break a lance **across** the counter, over a piece of cotton. Those ladies were outspoken, not like many of our friends now, who appear to be afraid to speak of unconditional reprobation. But those went the whole length,—'God decreed all things, whatsoever comes to pass.' 'Then, madam, there can be no such thing as sin in the universe, for whatsoever God decrees is right; nor can there be such a place as you call hell, for if God has decreed that you should go to Heaven and I to hell, I am fulfilling his will as completely as you are. There can be no worm there for **me**. I fall in with my Maker's plans. I am fulfilling His will, and the highest Seraph can do no more.' Those parties respected him, and frequently went to hear him preach.

"It required no small share of moral courage to receive the preachers in the Popish towns of Ireland, especially the Black Cap, or Cavalry Preachers, as the missionaries were called, because they generally wore a black handkerchief on their heads when preaching in the streets, and sometimes preached in the saddle; but when Ouseley came round—who was especially obnoxious to the priests and Papists—Mr. Gundy gave him the right hand of fellowship. He was a lover of good men, and the cause of God lay near his heart. Ouseley had a peculiar method of introducing religious topics into conversation. One day in the store he was talking to a young man on the subject of religion, a recruiting sergeant happened to pass at the time, and Ouseley asked—'Do you think, will that man get a pension?' 'Yes', said the young man, 'if he serves out his regular time.' 'Why?' said Ouseley. 'Because,' said he, 'he was regularly enlisted; he took the bounty; he learned the exercise; and he is actually in the King's service.' 'Ha! you booby,' said Ouseley, 'you were talking a while ago of your hopes of Heaven; but you

were never enlisted in the Royal army ; you never learned
the exercise ; you were never actually in the King's service, and still you are expecting a pension. The King
will say you are an impostor ; go away with you.'

" A great revival of religion took place on the circuit in
1838. Mr. Gundy took an active part in it, and many
were converted. Some are standing to this day, holding
prominent positions in the Church of God, and some
have passed through death triumphant home. After Mr.
Gundy's removal to Mt. Mellick, business increased very
rapidly, so much so, that he thought he was justified in
enlarging his business, which cost him a great deal of
money. He made heavy purchases, and prepared to do
a large business, but owing to a variety of causes which
need not here be enumerated, business became very dull.
It was a most trying season to business men, especially to
those of limited capital. Mr. Gundy, with several others,
had to succumb to the pressure of the times. He gave
up all to his creditors, barely keeping what would pay
the passage of his family to the new world. God opened
up his way into the ministry here, and, I believe, he was
respected and useful on all the circuits he travelled."

Mr. Gundy was strongly opposed to the doctrines and
usages of Popery. From his long and familiar acquaintance with the system in Ireland and elsewhere, he had
seen its workings only to be more thoroughly convinced
of its anti-christian motives and operations.

Some years after coming to this country, he united with
the Orangemen, out of pure sympathy with their publish-

ed objects, namely, to promote true morality, and true fidelity to God, and loyalty to the sovereign and laws of the British nation. I have often thought that, in this, he was led somewhat into error; for, while it could not more fully qualify him to promote morality and religion, it complicated him in the admixture of political questions more than perhaps would, in other men, have been safe for a Methodist preacher.

No system of organized opposition could more fully acquaint him with the errors of Popery, or make him more strongly determined to oppose them. He was, no doubt, influenced to this course by those whom he took to be friends, and perhaps they were so. However, in the exercise of his deliberate judgment, he was not only connected with the Orangemen in name, but, until lately, he attended regularly their meetings, and used his influence in private and public to further their objects; and, if I am not mistaken, was for several years elected to the position of grand chaplain of the order in this Province. He frequently preached for them on their assembling to commemorate the battle of the Boyne; but, while he gave thanks to Providence for the blessings of deliverance from the rule of Popery, he never forgot to point his hearers to the simple Gospel, with its simple yet effective plan of salvation, for a personal meetness for hope on earth and fruition in Heaven. He was an ardent lover of his native land, and, like the afflicted Jew, mourned over the desolations made by sin, and rightly saw in Popery Ireland's greatest trouble, and the source of the ig-

norance and immorality of such vast numbers **of her**
people. This, however, seems characteristic of the Irishman, educated or uneducated ; and although, from a
knowledge of its history, it may appear strange that such
love of country should prevail, yet so it is. The Roman
Catholicism of Ireland has been its bane,—the true Gospel must be the source of its salvation. Ireland ! wretched, unhappy Ireland ! when will thy miseries cease ? One
can scarcely write upon a subject so closely allied to Ireland's history without yielding to the temptation to glance
at those miseries, and suggest their cure. Her history is
a very checkered one. She has been the hot-bed of both
political and religious strife for ages, and it seems to be
her lot still to suffer from foes without and fears within.
There are characteristics attaching to her people which,
if guided into proper channels, would constitute her **one**
of the happiest and most prosperous portions of the British Dominions. But alas for Ireland ; she seems doomed
to a perpetual warfare. Her years have been devoted to developing "the works of the flesh" instead of
multiplying "the fruits of the spirit." Why this is so,
her over-sanguine and incredulous people are slow to
learn. Seditions, envyings, revellings, murders, and such
like, have apparently been allowed full sway, with little,
if any, let or hindrance. The germ of true patriotism is,
however, not wanting in many of her sons, and **the seeds**
of many noble qualities are evidently laid in her soil ; **yet**
some heavy incubus is staying the wheels of her prosperity,—some dark cloud, like a pall of death, is settled over

K

her. The genius of no nation can ever exceed her spirit of philanthropy, or rise higher than her well-springs of benevolence. The love of home and country, possessed by her people, cannot be well surpassed, and there seems very little of natural quality wanting to make her fields and workshops, and all her departments of industry, to bring forth plentifully ; and yet, perhaps, there are few civilized nations that have less of this, while few, if any, cost more for the administration of justice ; and even then the turbulent passions of her masses can scarcely be controlled. There are, however, many noble exceptions to this rule. Possessed of the finest intellect, many of her sons have risen to fill offices of trust and responsibility abroad, and, not able to rule themselves, they have gone to assist other nations to the success they should have expected at home. Many of Ireland's most talented sons have supposed they saw the cause of her failures, first in one department and then in another. One thought the evil lay in a want of proper political rights, and he set about correcting the evil; another saw the difficulty to arise from a defective educational **system,** and reforms in this department were introduced. And, in whatever direction the effort was put forth, all seems to have been as yet unsuccessful in raising Ireland to the proud position she is ambitious to gain. Fenianism, foul child of the devil, under pretence of seeking the distressed country's good is only subjecting her to greater trouble, and few, very few of her own people, seem to have found the real cause of Ireland's difficulty, and this is the wonder. In her subjection to Rome, evidently lies the secret of **her sorrow, for her** people, naturally religious, **and the** uneducated **part of** them much inclined to superstition, **she has fallen an easy** prey to the awful system of Popery. **In becoming the** dupe and vassal of the Roman Pontiff, she has laid herself under perpetual obligation of the **most** humiliating kind. She has been bound hand and foot, soul and body, night and day, to yield her resources and affections to a foreign Potentate, until she has increased her bondage and complicated her troubles.

None of the dependencies of Great Britain have **ever** received so much government support ; **none have** cost nearly so much for military and constabulary force ; none have ever received so much monetary assistance at various times as this country, and yet not one of the colonies has the same state of dwarfishness or has given half the trouble as has this little " sea girt isle."* **There** must be a reason for this state of things. I am persuaded the spring of her miseries lies in the God-dishonouring and priest-elevating character of her religion.

---

* See Ireland's Miseries, Cause and Cure, by Dr. Dill ; and Thom's Statistics for 1852, page 257.

CHAPTER XIV.

THE PROTESTANTISM OF IRELAND—POPERY IRELAND'S
MISERY—THE GOSPEL HER ONLY HOPE.

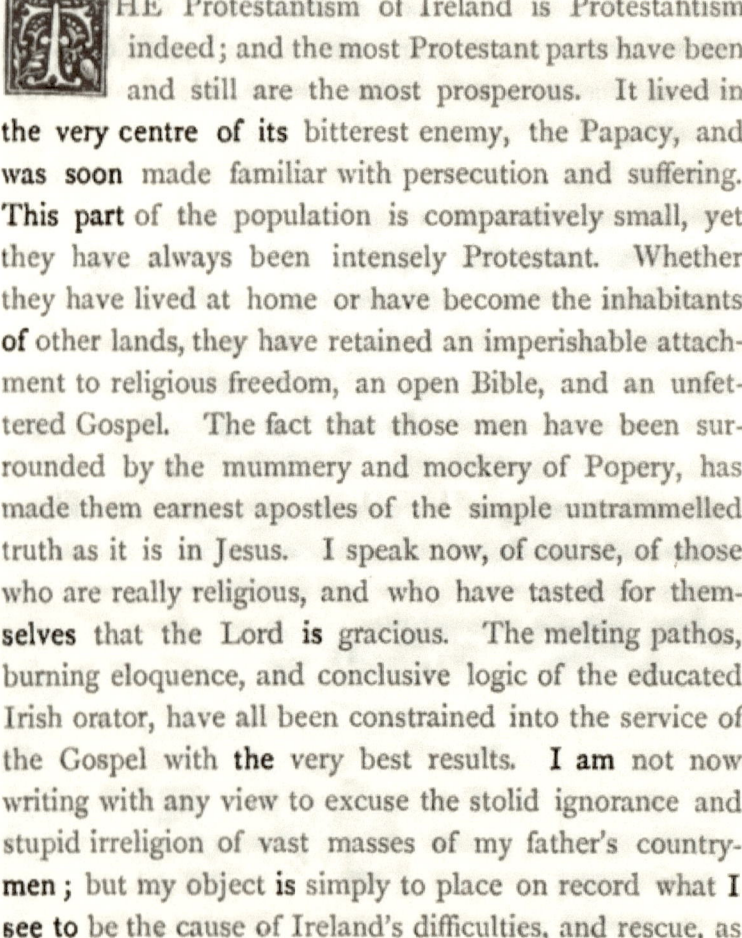HE Protestantism of Ireland is Protestantism
indeed; and the most Protestant parts have been
and still are the most prosperous. It lived in
the very centre of its bitterest enemy, the Papacy, and
was soon made familiar with persecution and suffering.
This part of the population is comparatively small, yet
they have always been intensely Protestant. Whether
they have lived at home or have become the inhabitants
of other lands, they have retained an imperishable attachment to religious freedom, an open Bible, and an unfettered Gospel. The fact that those men have been surrounded by the mummery and mockery of Popery, has
made them earnest apostles of the simple untrammelled
truth as it is in Jesus. I speak now, of course, of those
who are really religious, and who have tasted for themselves that the Lord is gracious. The melting pathos,
burning eloquence, and conclusive logic of the educated
Irish orator, have all been constrained into the service of
the Gospel with the very best results. I am not now
writing with any view to excuse the stolid ignorance and
stupid irreligion of vast masses of my father's countrymen; but my object is simply to place on record what I
see to be the cause of Ireland's difficulties, and rescue, as

far as possible, the natural qualities of the heart and the general character of the Irishman, as such, from the universal stigma under which they rest. His natural endowments I believe to be good, his associations unfortunate. Like the poor African, where slavery exists, it is hard for him, unless he is more than human, to surmount all difficulties, and stand amongst men to take rank with the foremost. I have said that Popery is the source of Ireland's evils, and so it is. Are the people ignorant? They are made so by this "sum of all villanies." Are they superstitious? They were educated in it through the influence of this degrading system. To think of curing her ills or remedying her evils through simple legislation, or the mere influence of any system of secular education, is preposterous. Nothing but the promotion of true religion can overthrow her enemies or shake off her chains of bondage.

It seems to me that the Christian world should turn its attention more fully to this field for missionary labour. Once relieve Ireland from the thraldom of the Papacy, and she will soon throw off the bondage of sin, with the innumerable evils which at present crush her to the earth; and the natural warm-heartedness and active brains of her people will then soon raise her to her true position and make her prosperous in piety, as she will be growing in natural resources. Ireland loved Rome better than she did her own sons; and, in obedience to this foreign spiritual Potentate, she hugged the chains of her bondage. There is no wonder, therefore, that she is now reaping the fruit in the material destitution, which corresponds with the spiritual degeneracy of her people. Every country to which Rome has been attached, and in which the poisonous vapours of her religious breath have been felt, has evidently laboured under the curse of God and the ban of enlightened humanity, and they have never known anything like material or intellectual promotion.

Spain, France, Austria and Ireland, of the Eastern hemisphere, and Mexico and the Spanish possessions of South America on the Western, have all been stunted in their moral and material growth; while Great Britain, Scotland, Prussia, Switzerland, and Norway of the Eastern, and Canada and the United States of America on the Western hemisphere, living in the enjoyment of an enlightened Gospel ministry, and in daily communion with the Father of Spirits, through an open Bible, have gone forward in the march of greatness.

"Rome eclipses the mind, corrupts the conscience, destroys the heart, debases the whole nature, blasts man's temporal interests, and clouds his eternal prospects."*

The heavens above are moved, and the earth beneath is trembling with the mighty commotions caused by the conflicting elements of good and evil; while the face of a holy, but justly indignant God, is set against the horrid blasphemies and hateful hypocrisies done in this world under the garb of religion. Within the last few months, what wonders have been wrought by the hand of Divine Providence towards the overthrow of the monstrous sys-

---

* Dr. Dill's work, page 98-186.

tem of Popery! Italy, that once lay at the feet of the
Papacy, has burst the chains which bound her. Spain,
once the most obedient servant of his Holiness, has,
within an incredibly short space of time, made a successful effort to control her own affairs, and has lately called
to her throne a liberal prince—son of the excommunicated
Victor Emmanuel. France, only a short time ago ruled
by "the fairest son of the Church," has been humbled at
the feet of Protestant Prussia, her late emperor a homeless
wanderer, and the whole country forced to submit to
terms dictated by her successful antagonist. The Pope
himself is merely tolerated in his spiritual authority in
Rome, where he *had* his throne and the seat of his
strength, and from whence he hurled the thunders of the
Vatican; and all this is more wonderful when we remember that, in imposing upon the ignorant submission of his
devotees, his Holiness yielded to the proud ambition of
a wicked heart; and, by the consent of his clerical representatives from all nations, capped the climax of impiety
and human assumption by declaring himself infallible.
If these events and many more of a similar character,
which might be referred to, do not indicate the speedy
overthrow of this entire system of religious mockery, then
I am altogether astray in reading the signs of the times.

At all events the way has now been so opened up
that, unprotected by the strong military powers which
once sustained this Church, she will be compelled to contest every inch of ground with those who labour to circu-
late in every country, and put in the hands of every man,

an open Bible.   Rome can no longer successfully close
that book, or insist on her own interpretation, while the
military power to enforce this is wanting.   The dark ages
for the world, we trust, are forever past, and, if systems of
darkness and error will remain, they must do so in face
of the fact that " the true light *now shineth*."   The con-
vents and nunneries of Rome must be unlocked, and the
light of day will shine into them, and as Luther grasped,
with all the avidity of a starving man, the truths of the
chained Bible at Erfurt, so hundreds and thousands
of the poor deluded devotees of Rome will reach out the
hand of **faith** to catch the life-giving words of the missionary message to the world.   It is a coincidence no less
pleasing than wonderful that, when the Italian troops
entered Rome, the man who led them into the gates was
an humble colporteur, clothed with Divine authority, with
an open Bible in his hand, crying, " Rome for Christ !
Rome for Christ."   Happy augury this for the future !
If the Bible, instead of the Papacy, had ruled Rome for the
last few centuries, how much ignorance, superstition and
crime would it have saved the world ?   She has been the
prolific source of darkness and spiritual bondage to the
nations.   Here is where the erroneous dogmas of the
priests first had an existence ; here is where began the in-
quisition ; where was concocted the scheme of the invin-
cible Armada ; and here, in short, is the seat of the beast,
and the residence of the mother of harlots.   There has
been more perversion and prostitution of truth carried on
in Rome than in any other city of the world ; and that

all under the profession of giving light to the people on the very questions which, within her walls, are being shrouded in impenetrable darkness. There is no wonder, therefore, that, in yielding allegiance to Rome, Ireland has crippled her energies, and made her sons an easy prey to wicked and designing men, and, in her folly and madness, has brought herself to believe a lie, and to work all manner of evil with greediness.

We again affirm the Gospel, the unadulterated, unfettered Gospel, must be the means of rescuing unhappy Ireland from her enemy. Her people must be made to feel that the malady is a spiritual one, and can only be cured by genuine spiritual remedies. There is a large amount of natural talent in the Irishman, a mental restlessness which will not allow him to be idle. If you do not furnish him with healthy literature and sound morality, he will procure and give currency to the unhealthy and unsound. Methodism in Ireland bears a very small **proportion** to the rest of the population, yet Methodism and Presbyterianism have done more than any other agencies for the elevation of her people. And to show that this unhappy country possesses a large amount of native talent, which may some day be more effectively used to her temporal and spiritual advantage, I may be allowed to say that the Methodism of Ireland has furnished some of the ablest preachers to her fields of labour, in all her Missionary work over the face of the globe. It is also surprising to note what a large proportion of the regular ministry of all churches in this, and almost all other countries, is either directly, or by ancestry, from the Emerald Isle. If, therefore, Ireland is to be rescued from the Papacy, she must be *filled* with the influences of an earnest Christianity. Then will she shine resplendent with the glory of a pure and holy life. The different branches of Christ's Church must be united in their efforts to hold forth, as at once, the healing medicine and the great physician, "Jesus Christ, and Him crucified." Dr. Dill, in the closing pages of his eloquently written work says, "If ever there was a work which pre-eminently required the Spirit of Christ on the part, both of churches and ministers, it is ours. Perhaps there is not beneath the sun a field of labour in which one is more forcibly taught the utter impotence of human effort, and the special need of Divine aid. 'Tis here we are made to feel the whole force of the sublime but humbling sentiment, 'Not by might, nor by power, but by my Spirit, saith the Lord;' and persuaded we are that every requisite to secure triumphant success, even in it, is *more deep-toned apostolic piety*. What we chiefly want is that unquenchable spirit of love to Jesus, and to souls, which **glowed** in the breast of a Paul and a John. This would give us men, and constrain our ablest ministers, instead of aspiring to the highest places in the church, to envy the missionary his hard lot, and say, 'Here am I, Lord, send me.'"

The importance of the subject must be my only **apology** for this lengthy digression. It would be a matter of unspeakable joy to my dear father-in-law were he permitted to know of the recent changes which have taken place in the lessening of Popish influence throughout the nations of the earth, and would, no doubt, be regarded as the harbinger of better days to oppressed humanity.

Mr. Gundy hated no man ; his opposition was against the system, while he pitied the men who were its dupes and vassals.

He was a good man, an humble Christian, a true *Protestant*, a faithful minister, a loving partner, parent and friend, while he clung to Christ as the only ground of his hope of Heaven, and the source of his success on earth. " He walked with God, and had this testimony that he pleased God ; and he was not, for God took him."

> " How beautiful it is for man to die
> Upon the Walls of Zion ! to be call'd
> Like a watch-worn and weary sentinel,
> To put his armour off, and rest—in heaven !"

CHAPTER XV.

MR. GUNDY AS A MAN—HIS HABITS OF LIVING—VIEWED
AS A PREACHER, ETC.—TESTIMONIALS OF REV. J. CAS-
WELL AND DR. COCKER.

MR. GUNDY was possessed of a fine, healthy constitution ; and he scarcely ever knew what it was to be sick. His energies of body, which were always more or less accustomed to active labor, were preserved with unusual freshness until his seventy-fifth year. Perhaps his habits of cleanliness contributed much to this, as also his accustomed cold bath every morning, winter and summer, during nearly his whole life. He was very regular and orderly in his habits, and must have a place for everything, and everything must be in its place. Thus by constant care, and by strictly temperate conduct in all things, he was, at the age of seventy-four years, a hale, fresh-looking, and amiable old man. He had a very evenly balanced mind, and the health of his body contributed to the harmony of his faculties, the freshness of his thought, and the spirit of liberal Christianity, which always marked his life. His mind was richly stored with truth from the fertile fields of science, but it was especially in theology that he seemed to delight. He regarded John Wesley and Dr. Adam Clarke as model men in many respects ; and the advice of these men he earnestly cherished and followed, as far as it was possible for him to do. In his reading, while he was strongly attached to one thorough system, he was no bigot on the one hand, or sceptic on the other. It was his practice carefully to weigh the thoughts of all the authors he read ; and, while he accepted that which commended itself to his judgment, he as freely rejected that which did not, no matter who was the author—friend or foe.

In our opinion, he was right in this, as none but a narrow mind can harbour bigotry, so none but a mind equally contracted can encourage infidelity.

His view of science and of art, and his knowledge of history and philosophy, only lifted his soul up towards Heaven in thankfulness that in them he could see the evidences of a Father's hand and a Father's heart. I have, however, no desire unduly to exalt him before the world, and must not, therefore, forget to inform my readers that he made no pretensions to high intellectual attainments.

He does not appear before us as a man of science, but as a man of God. His knowledge of the abstruse sciences was quite limited, and was gathered simply from reading the works of authors on the various subjects within the range of ordinary common sense men. He seldom speculated in the new theories which have occasionally startled the world. You have already been informed that his school-boy days were few, and those not favoured with the advantages of superior teachers. Under such circumstances, the ordinary intellect would have sought its sphere of thought amongst those whose daily employment is confined to the drudgery of manual labour ; but, blest with an active and more than ordinary sized brain, and guided by the hand of Providence, he rose step by step in the acquisition of knowledge every day. He was, therefore, as far as his mental strength or intellectual fitness for the "high calling" of a gospel minister is concerned, a self-taught and self-made man. His social qualities, if any-thing, were in advance of his intellectual. In the social circle, he was dearly beloved by all who knew him. Here he was gentlemanly and courteous, he was affable yet dig-nified; and he brought into this sphere the simplicity of a child and the mature thought of the man of God. He hated the churl, and in his heart despised the arrant trum-pery of the fop or buffoon. He made no pretentions to greatness, but, after all, he was great in his unassuming modesty and goodness of heart. He was friendly to all, and could receive abuse with meekness, but was incapa-ble of giving it. He was a true friend, and his memory seemed to be particularly tenacious of those with whom he had been familiarly acquainted.—A friend was never forgotten. In the family circle he was a favourite; and no man ever loved the sacred spot called home more than he, or took greater pains to make all happy who gathered round his hearthstone.

As a husband, he was kind, loving, faithful and atten-tive, and no woman ever had greater reason to love the partner of her joys and sorrows than Mrs. Gundy, and this she knew full well herself; and never was the confid-ing affection of a wife more nobly responded to than in her case. Their lives were truly linked together by the chain of love, and during a long and somewhat rough voyage over life's sea, they mutually sympathized with and supported each other. As a father, he was loving without being too indulgent ; he was firm, without severity ; and, making himself one with his children, he became the inspirer of their earthly happiness. Nothing could give him greater delight than to see his children walking in the truth. In a letter to one of his sons—then unconverted —he says :—" My dear son,—There is nothing like religion. I hope you will not rest without the love of God shed abroad in your heart, by the Holy Ghost given unto you. This blessing is obtained by repentance towards God, and simple faith in the Saviour. But you must pray, and pray in faith, nothing doubting, and while you are praying and believing, and thus resting your soul on the Saviour of mankind, you will obtain the pearl of great price. God grant it for Christ's sake." For this object he wrestled often, in prayer, with God ; for this he sought to guide them by precept, and lead by his example. His joy at realizing the conversion of all his children cannot be expressed in words. Every member of his family being converted to Christ, and on the way to heaven, could not do otherwise than make him doubly thankful to God for His mercy ; and, if a golden crown had been placed on his head, and he made the king of nations, he could not have been more the subject of glorious gratitude than when four of his sons, giving promise of usefulness, were brought forward by the church, and honoured with a position in the gospel ministry. John, the eldest, was called out by Dr. Richey the same year as himself ; Samuel, by the New Connexion, in 1853 ; James, in 1859, and Joseph, in 1860.   These, together with the father, presented a spectacle of family devotion over which an angel's mind might be filled with joy.   It has been remarked by those who witnessed the scene, that his face grew radiant with the glory of an inward gratitude, as they came, one after another, and were solemnly set apart to the work of the Lord ; and he often expressed his hope that the remaining son—William—might find in the same sphere a congenial employment for his powers.   His life was wrapt up in his family, and to have them travelling on the way to Heaven, was his highest ambition concerning them.   In short, he was a man of great simplicity of manner and evenness of mind ; and was always firm in the course he had chosen—to work for God.   If many a man had been in his place, he would have shrunk from the difficulties Mr. Grundy passed through, and, by the grace of God, overcame.   He scarcely ever knew, during all the twenty years of his ministry amongst us, what it was to get the whole of his salary—too small when all received.   Often he obtained no more than $100, together with some provisions for table use, for a year of toil and care.   But, in the midst of it all, he was not the man to murmur at the hardness of his lot.   He hopefully plodded on, and, by the mercy of God, came to an honoured grave and an eternal reward.

As a preacher, Mr. Gundy was what, in this age of Methodism, we would call one of the old style.   The embellishment of his sermon was its earnestness, while the great

fundamental doctrines of our religion formed its substance.   He gave great prominence to the *atonement*.
"Jesus Christ, by the grace of God, tasted death for every
man," contained the gist of his theme.   He dwelt principally
upon the doctrinal subjects, which he opened up to view
with great clearness and skill ; and applied them to the
hearts and consciences of his hearers with logical force and
conclusiveness.   He never preached a sermon without
having plenty of Christ in it.   Justification, regeneration
and sanctification were all realized through faith in His
blood.   He gave little or no attention to speculative
theories, and combatted false ones by faithfully preaching
" Christ Jesus and him crucified."   This is a grand theme,
and sublime indeed are those which cluster around and
are framed into it.

Truly sublime were the sentiments of his closing
sermon, although he was not aware it was to be his last.
It was founded upon the noble language of triumph
uttered by the Apostle Paul.

" I have fought a good fight, I have finished my course,
I have kept the faith : henceforth there is laid up for me
a crown of righteousness, which the Lord, the righteous
Judge, shall give me at that day : and not to me only,
but unto all them also that love his appearing."

No man could insist more strongly than he upon the
important doctrines of justification by faith and the witness of the Spirit, together with the advanced work of
sanctification by the Holy Ghost.   The importance of
these he pressed home upon the conscience, with strong

L

argument, and often with burning pathos, if not eloquence. He was opposed to a flowery and vapid production, both in conscience and capacity.   He invariably found it better to feed the souls of his hearers than tickle their fancy. However, there seemed to be, with him little, if any, choice in the matter, as his mind always ran in the direction of good solid ground for the sinner's reliance in hope of eternal life.   He held the doctrine of sanctification as a work distinct and separate from justification.   In short, he fully adopted Wesley's view of this question, and endeavoured to impress upon his hearers the importance of pushing forward to its attainment.   His reliance was upon the general argument given, which he considered sufficient to establish the doctrine as distinct, separate from, and subsequent to, justification.   Indeed, the more I know of his views of Scripture, and his style and manner of preaching, the more I see he held fully Wesley's sentiments as set forth in his published sermons, and accepted Wesley's suggestion as contained in the preface to the American edition of his works.   Mr. Gundy was highly respected in the conference, and where he was known in the Connexion.   I have no doubt but he would have been honoured with the president's chair, but for the fact of an unfitness for it, arising from a partial deafness which had followed him for many years of his life.   He, however, was frequently chairman of a district, and, so far as he was personally concerned, he had all the honour he desired, in the *exalted position* of a faithful, accredited and useful minister of Jesus Christ.

But he has gone from us forever, **and** we shall no more hear his familiar voice, **or** be charmed onward by his smile ; but we may be lured towards Heaven **by his holy** life, and **stimulated in the** service of Jesus by his noble **example.**

Mr. Gundy did not sparkle as a star of the first magnitude, but he shone **in** the firmament of the church with a clear and even brightness. He was not a flower of rarest kind, **whose varied tints and** hues were incomparably beautiful ; but the fragrance of his life will never die. He was not a great man, and laid no claim to superior ability as a scholar or preacher ; but in the everyday faithfulness and plodding industry of his life, few surpassed him. **He** was a man of prayer, and often drew the inspiration of his happy life from his close intimacy with the throne of grace. His mind was on his work, and nothing else ; and he never made use of the holy office to promote **his** own pleasure **or** increase his wealth. Having enough to supply the present wants of the body, he was contented and happy, and, by rigid economy, he was enabled to save a little for his declining days, which, together with his annuity, raised him above the inconvenience and suffering of want, or the mere dependence on friends, however kind. But he is gone, and we miss him very much **in the** family, and his aged partner from her side ; and, as a Connexion, at our annual gatherings, we will miss his hoary head, and venerable form, and **pleasant smile, and the warm grasp** of his hand, accompanied with **the familiar words, "** I hope you 're very well." And we

will miss him, too, from the solemn scenes of our conference sacramental service ; but he has gone from the
church below to join the church above. May we meet
him there.

I may be pardoned for introducing here the tribute to
his memory contained in the following letters of condol-
ence, received after his departure. The first from the
Rev. James Caswell ; the other from the Rev. William
Cocker, D.D. :—

"I deeply sympathize with his bereaved widow and
sorrowing family, but they have the satisfaction of know-
ing that he died in the Lord ; that he left behind him
an unstained character, and unspotted reputation. A
purer, more unselfish, or even-minded man, I presume,
hardly ever lived. His is a fragrant memory ; one that
his children and grand-children, and brethren in the ministry and the church he so long and so faithfully served,
will be proud of and thankful for."

Dr. Cocker says : "It seems to me that your cup of
sorrow has all the sweetening elements and influences
that we can hope for in this imperfect state. Your beloved
father lived to a good old age—lived to exemplify Christian
graces in the family circle, to turn many to righteousness
by his ministerial labors ; and now he has gone to enjoy
the reward of a 'good and faithful servant,' and to 'shine
as the stars forever and ever.' May we all be enabled to
follow him in the paths of holiness and usefulness that
we may join with his glorified spirit amidst the exercises
and pleasures of the better land."

With the following lines, communicated to the *Evangelical Witness*, by the friend, whose initials are given below, we close this short and imperfect sketch of the life of one whom we expect again to see, and with whom we hope to join in celebrating the praises of the Redeemer, throughout the endless ages of eternity :—

IN MEMORIAM.

REV. WILLIAM GUNDY.

Simple and lowly as a little child,
Sitting with Mary at the Master's feet ;
Nathaniel-like, there lurked no base deceit
　　Within thy soul, that in transparence smiled,
　　Nor heresy, nor schism thee defiled.
Truth's champion in a bold, blaspheming age,
To a false reading of the Sacred Page,
　　No sophistry thy upright mind beguiled.

Shepherd belov'd, with tender, yearning heart,
Seeking the sheep that in the cloudy day
Had wandered from the heavenly fold away :
　　Oh, who, save One, may gauge aright its smart ?
Sense, wondering, asks, " Who, who thy place can fill ?"
Faith's motto is " Jehovah Jireh " still !

J. E.

SUBSTANCE OF A SERMON PREACHED IN THE M. N. C.
CHURCH, MILTON, JUNE 23RD, 1870, BY THE REV.
JAMES M'ALISTER, ON THE OCCASION OF THE DEATH
OF REV. WILLIAM GUNDY.

(" Only brief notes of the discourse were in manuscript
when it was delivered, hence, when asked by the author
of this memoir to furnish it for publication, it was with
some hesitancy we complied.   We have gleaned from the
notes and from memory, as best we could, the principal
parts of the sermon, and earnestly hope its perusal may
be blest to those who read it.")

———

*O death, where is thy sting ?   O grave, where is thy
victory ?   The sting of death is sin; and the strength of
sin is the law.   But thanks be to God, which giveth us the
victory through our Lord Jesus Christ.*—1st COR. xv., 55,
56 and 57.

THE glorious doctrine of the resurrection, so ably
and beautifully discussed in this chapter, is the
most important of our holy' religion.   It lies at
the very foundation of the Christian system.   Hence the
Apostle tells the Corinthians that this was among the
first doctrines which he preached unto them, which they
also had received, and by which they were saved; and
as this doctrine was of such importance, he proceeds to
show them that it rested on the clearest evidence.   Christ

having been seen after his resurrection by Cephas, then of the twelve, after that by over five hundred; then of James, afterwards by all the Apostles; and, last of all, by himself. At the time, therefore, when the Apostle wrote this Epistle, there must have been some three hundred living witnesses, who were ready to testify that they had seen Christ alive after his death and resurrection. Now, if in the mouth of two or three witnesses every word is to be established, surely two or three hundred should settle the matter, and place it beyond dispute; especially so, if we remember that this testimony was borne in the face of strong opposition, and that on the side of the opposition there was wealth and power. The rulers, both in church and state, being allied in their vindictive hatred of this truth, would have charged the Apostles with libel, and in their courts of justice would have proved them guilty of falsehood and deception, and have punished them accordingly. The fact that they never attempted such a course, shows that they knew the truths set forth by the Apostles could not be proven false. Hence, too, the boldness of the Apostles in proclaiming these doctrines everywhere, and challenging investigation.

Paul felt the importance and value of this doctrine under consideration, for he tells the Corinthians that if it were false, all was lost; his, and the other Apostles' preaching was **vain**; and the faith of those who believed this gospel was without foundation—all was a vain delusion. **It is,** therefore, a matter of great joy to us that there is no room for a reasonable doubt, or rationable objection to this doctrine.

In this chapter the Apostle takes up and treats the whole subject under four heads:—

1st. The fact itself. This he proves from scripture testimony, from Christ's resurrection, which, we have seen, rests on the most conclusive evidence ; and from the consequences of the contrary view, crushing out **every** aspiration after immortality, and blasting every hope of an hereafter which God has implanted in our nature.

2nd. He replies to the objector's query, ver. 35, "How are **the** dead raised up, and with what body do they come ?" This he does by referring to facts which are patent in nature in the vegetable and animal kingdoms ; and also makes the starry arch tributary to his argument, furnishing him with beautiful illustrations of his theme.

3rd. He shows what will become of the living at the sound of the last trump. They shall be changed, putting on incorruption and immortality in a moment, and

4th. The glorious issues flowing out of this doctrine, and the practical bearings it should have on our lives. To this last division our text belongs ; and we can contemplate it to-day with joy over the lifeless form of our departed brother, because we have the assurance that he was a sharer of this victory and triumph. Let us contemplate,—

I. The *foes* presented to us in the text—*death* and the *grave.*

These are two-fold. **They are** personified and repre-

sented as in close and inseparable alliance.   Death kills
and the grave stands ready to swallow up his victims.
Such are the consequences almost immediately following
the stroke of death, that the most beloved objects of our
lives have to be yielded up to the grave.   Yea, even **the**
beloved Sarah becomes loathsome, and Abraham, though
he loved her so ardently, has to seek a place where she
may be buried out of his sight.   Death attacks in many
terrible forms.   Sometimes with measured tread, with
stealthy step, he "comes up into our windows."   And
again, suddenly seizing his victims, he sweeps them away
as with a whirlwind.   Sometimes revelling in the pestilence and famine—these mighty agents of his—depopu-
lating towns, cities and countries, disregarding rank, sex,
age or condition, spreading alarm on every hand.   Sometimes the sword is unsheathed, and then a nation mourns
its slain.   While the grave's capacious maw swallows up
death's victims sometimes in heaps, yet never saying
enough.   And again, the greedy sea affords concealment
to the fallen, not allowing the **mourners** the pleasant,
though sad and painful, duty of erecting the marble slab
to mark the last resting place of loved ones.   O what
devastation and havoc have these monsters made among
our race.

Death is armed with a terrible sting, dagger or goad,
by which he **is** continually urging on the generations of
men, till they fall into his empire—the grave—to which
victory is attributed.   Having overcome and conquered all
human life, with two exceptions, he reigns victorious, and

stands like a mighty monarch swaying his sceptre over the quiet inhabitants of his domain.

The text tells us the sting of death is sin; it is this that has introduced death into the world—this that gives him power to carry on his work of destruction; and, by sin, both the bodies and souls of men are slain. "The strength of sin is the law." The law pronounces the sentence of death, "The soul that sinneth shall die ;" and, if nothing else interpose, the sinner must remain forever under the empire of death.

"The law gives sin its damning power." "I was alive without the law once," says the apostle; "but, when the law came, sin revived and I died;" hence the strength of sin is the law. We see, then, that these two foes have had extensive, indiscriminate, and universal triumph over the generations of men, and this renders them terrible. Surely a victory over such foes must be glorious ! This brings us to contemplate—

II. Second, the victory given us by the resurrection over these foes.

Thank God, life and immortality have been brought to light by the Gospel. These allied foes, death and the grave, are overcome, robbed of their terror, shall be of their spoil, and prostrate, dethroned and left without an empire here, they shall be banished to their native hell. Christ Jesus has "abolished death." He is "The resurrection and the life ;" and, however killed or wherever buried, "All shall come forth ;" for, "As in Adam all die, even so in Christ shall all be made alive." The Son of

God was manifest, that he might destroy the works of the
devil.   This was a principal part of Satan's work to intro-
duce sin and death into our earth, and it is an important
part of Christ's work to counteract and destroy both ;
hence, in his whole history, we find the Saviour manifest-
ing a deep interest in this achievement.   Centuries before
his incarnation, looking out from the bosom of the Father
and contemplating this victory, we hear him exclaim, " I
will ransom them from the power of the grave ; I will
redeem them from death : O death, I will be thy plagues ;
O grave, I will be thy destruction."   While he dwelt
among men, he often spoke of death and the grave, as
though they had no existence.   "Whosoever liveth and
believeth in me, shall never die."   In speaking of the
death of Lazarus, he said, "Our friend Lazarus sleepeth."
Thus, in view of the resurrection, death is compared to a
sleep ; repeatedly is this Christian name applied to death;
we are not to sorrow as those who have no hope for our
friends who sleep in Jesus.

> "Asleep in Jesus, blessed sleep,
>   From which none ever wake to weep."

Does the mother, as she lays away her babe and im-
prints on its lips the good-night kiss, mourn it as lost?
Nay, she thinks of it coming forth in the morning, refreshed and invigorated after the repose of the night ;
and so the Christian mourns not departed friends as lost,
but looks forward to the resurrection morn, when " This
corruptible shall have put on incorruption, and this mortal
shall have put on immortality ;"

> "And every form and every face
> Look heavenly and divine."

For, "Having borne the image of the earthy, we shall also bear the image of the heavenly." The Saviour is still anticipating the final consummation of this part of his work. Paul tells the Hebrew Christians that Christ, having "offered one sacrifice for sins forever, sat down on the right hand of God; from henceforth expecting till his enemies be made his footstool." In this chapter we are told He must reign till he has put all enemies under his feet. The last enemy that shall be destroyed is death. Thus we see that, while "The wages of sin is death, the gift of God is eternal life, through Jesus Christ our Lord." Death is robbed of his sting, the grave of its terror ; and, in many of its aspects, the curse is turned into a blessing, death being forced to act as the agent to release God's children from pain and sorrow, and admit them to happiness and joy ; and the grave the place where, like the caterpillar as a worm after its long sleep, comes forth the beautiful butterfly ; so "Man sleeps a worm ; but wakes an angel." "Sown in dishonour, raised in glory." Precious, glorious doctrine, we press it with joy to our hearts, rejoicing to know that death is swallowed up in victory. "Thanks be to God who giveth us the victory through our Lord Jesus Christ." We remark—

III. This victory is God's gift to us, through our Lord Jesus Christ.

God is its author, and to Him the praise is due. No other being could overcome such terrible foes. He formed the plan, although, in its execution, he had to give His well beloved Son. Seeing our wretched and lost condition, His sympathies were called forth, and His great love, wherewith He loved us, manifested—and a theme of wonder and adoration for men and angels revealed, and a subject of praise for time and eternity given. We wonder at and admire this love, and angels desire to look into it, it is so deep that even angelic minds cannot fathom it, and the great multitude before the throne, which no man can number, make it the burden of their song. "Salvation to our God, which sitteth upon the throne, and unto the Lamb," is their theme, while we, in the church militant, sing also, ": Thanks be unto God, who giveth us the victory." By His almighty power He has overcome death and the grave for us.

It is through our Lord Jesus Christ, through His atoning blood, for "Without shedding of blood is no remission of sins," hence He took upon Him our nature. The Lord of life and glory became veiled in flesh ; to Him our nature was a garb of suffering. He put it on, says one, "That when the crisis of our redemption came, Justice might find Him attired and ready for the altar, a substance that his sword could smite, a victim that could agonize and bleed and die." Yes, "He, by the grace of God, tasted death for every man," and this gift of God is eternal life, or victory through our Lord Jesus Christ.

Not only are we saved by His glorious death, but also

through his powerful resurrection, "He died for our sins, and rose again for our justification." We have not to go to the tomb to find our glorious deliverer, He is not there, He is risen, and in His resurrection we see a guarantee of ours. He is the first fruits ; He met death on his own domain, conquered him there, robbed him of his power, extracted his sting, disrobed him of his terror, threw open the gates of his prison, and left the monster scathed, enfeebled and prostrate at His feet. "Having spoiled principalities and powers, He made a show of them openly, triumphing over them."

> " The Saviour rose triumphant o'er the tomb,
> Light kindled in each grave and cheered the gloom,
> Death felt the mortal blow, and owned his fate ;
> Rent were his chains, flung wide his prison gate.
> Nor was the monster left himself unscathed—
> His sting was plucked, and low his power was laid,--
> In turn he was a helpless captive bound,
> To meet his sentence when the trump shall sound.

> " Then roll ye spheres and bring the triumph nigh,
> When man shall ever live and death shall die !
> The Saviour shall again his power reveal,
> And Satan's head again his tread shall feel,
> His voice the slumbers of the tomb shall break,
> And all the sleeping dead shall then awake,
> And he shall see his soul's enlarged desire,
> And *death* shall on the point of *truth* expire."

Through His atoning death and powerful resurrection, grace is given as we need it, the promised comforter has been sent to solace the dying Christian, and hope lights up his passage to and through the grave. He is supported by the assurance that his elder brother was there before him, that Jesus, his friend and his Saviour, passed through its portals for him, and now that Saviour has the keys of death and hell. These thoughts afford him joy and victory in the hour of dissolution, and "Death becomes the crown of life." "I congratulate you and myself," said John Foster, "that life is passing fast away. What a superlatively grand and consoling idea is that of death! Without this radiant idea, this delightful morning star, indicating that the luminary of eternity is going to rise, life would, to my view, darken into midnight melancholy. Oh, the expectation of living *here* and living *thus* always would be, indeed, a prospect of overwhelming despair. But thanks be to that fatal decree that dooms us to die! Thanks to that gospel which opens the vision of an endless life! And thanks, above all, to that Saviour friend who has promised to conduct all the faithful through the sacred trance of death into scenes of paradise and everlasting delight." Our blessed Redeemer fought the battle on earth, and won the victory here for us, but on the resurrection morn He shall celebrate His triumph, and exhibit our glorified bodies as trophies won from death and the grave. Our departed friend and brother will doubtless be among those trophies.

A few remarks regarding the deceased may now be in place. We all remember his meek, childlike, uncomplaining disposition. When he entered our ranks, there were causes of complaint that do not now exist. Then circuits were large, while remuneration was comparatively small; still he murmured not. Had he been a fault-finder we would not have before us to-day what we see, and what is almost without a parallel, four sons and one son-in-law, all ministers of the Gospel, and thus following in the footsteps of a revered father. Well we remember what joy and satisfaction lit up the countenance of our departed friend, as he saw one after another of his sons consecrated to God, and to the work of the ministry. Now he rests from his labours, and his works follow him.

O may the mantles of our ascending Elijahs fall upon the Elishas that remain !

To the chief mourners I would just say, in conclusion, let the subject afford you comfort and consolation in this hour of your sorrow. Your partner, parent, friend is not lost, but gone before, hence you sorrow not as those who have no hope. He sleeps in Jesus. God spared him to you for a long time. You had his counsel and support in childhood, when you needed it most. You had the pleasure and privilege of ministering to him in his old age and feebleness. You have the strongest ground to hope that the glorious truths in our text cheered him in death, that he participated in this victory, and now is "forever with the Lord." Let it be your chief ambition to follow him as he followed Christ, and soon you shall be re-united in the presence of God, where there is no sorrow, no pain, no death ; the former things having passed away forever.

THE END.

James Campbell & Son's

CATALOGUE OF

SABBATH SCHOOL LIBRARIES.

No.

103.—The Evergreen Library 9 vols. $1 13.

60.—Valley of Blessing Library. 5 vols. $1 25.

87.—A. L. O. E. Library. 10 vols $1 25.

44.—Select Sunday School Library. 13 vols. $1 50.

7.—Alice Shaw Books. 10 vols. Hlf. bnd. $1 75.

8.—Favourite Library. 10 vols. Hlf. bnd. $1 75.

9.—Leigh Richmond Books. 10 vols. Hlf. bound, $1 75.

59.—Christian Hero Library. 6 vols. $1 50.

78.—Truth's Always best Library. 5 vols. $2 00.

85.—A. L. O. E. Library. 5 vols. $2 00.

104.—Sunny Scenes Library. 11 vols. $2 20.

64.—Eminent Christian. 4 vols. Hlf. bound, $2 40.

86.—A. L. O. E. Library. 5 vols. $2 50.

66.—Goodname. 9 vols. Hlf. bound, $2 40.

19.—Lily Douglas Books. 10 vols. Hlf. bnd, $2 75.

20.—Little Pansy Books. 10 vols. Hlf. bnd. $2 75.

84.—The Hidden Treasure. 7 vols. $2 50.

55.—The Red Velvet Bible Books. 7 vols. $2 50.

18.—The Home Library. 7 vols. Hlf. bound, $3.

83.—Cheerful Giver. 23 vol: Hlf. bound, $4 50,

57.—Commandment with Promise. 13 vols. $3 50.

45.—Select Sunday School. 30 vols. Hlf. bnd. $4.

No.

35.—Select Sunday School. 20 vols. Hlf. bound, $4 50.

36.—Select Sunday School. 20 vols. Hlf. bound, $4 50.

41.—Select Sunday School. 13 vols. Hlf. bound, $4 50.

27.—Select Sunday School. 30 vols. Hlf. bound, $4 50.

21.—"Across the River." 13 vols. $5 20.

49.—Select Sunday School. 20 vols. Hlf. bound, $5 50.

37.—Select Sunday School. 20 vols. Hlf. bound, $5 50.

38.—Select Sunday School. 20 vols. Hlf. bound, $5 50.

39.—Select Sunday School. 20 vols. Hlf. bound, $5 50.

40.—Select Sunday School. 20 vols. Hlf. bound, $5 50.

29.—Select Sunday School. 20 vols. $5.

67.—Old Humphrey. 24 vols. Hlf. bound, $5 50.

33.—Select Sabbath School. 48 vols. $6.

63.—Songs in the Night. 12 vols. Hlf. bnd. $6 50.

90.—Tales of my Sunday Scholars. 15 vols. Half bound, $6 50.

34.—The Young Teacher's Library. 25 vols. $6 25.

30.—Select Sunday School. 50 vols. Hlf. bnd. $8·

32.—Select Sunday School. 50 vols. Hlf. bnd. $10.

42.—Select Sabbath School. 50 vols. Hlf. bnd. $10.

68.—Temperance Library. 19 vols. $4 00.

70.—Temperance Library. 12 vols. $6 00.